Janet Little

Poetical Works of Janet Little

The Scotch Milkmaid

Janet Little

Poetical Works of Janet Little
The Scotch Milkmaid

ISBN/EAN: 9783337397883

Printed in Europe, USA, Canada, Australia, Japan

Cover: Foto ©Andreas Hilbeck / pixelio.de

More available books at **www.hansebooks.com**

THE

POETICAL WORKS

OF

JANET LITTLE,

THE

SCOTCH MILKMAID,

———•◆•———

A I R:

PRINTED BY JOHN & PETER WILSON,

M,DCC,XCII.

TO THE

RIGHT HONOURABLE

FLORA,

COUNTESS OF LOUDOUN,

THE FOLLOWING

POEMS

ARE

WITH PERMISSION,

HUMBLY INSCRIBED,

BY

YOUR LADYSHIP'S]

EVER GRATEFUL,

AND OBEDIENT

HUMBLE SERVANT,

CONTENTS.

A 3

✦

CONTENTS.

SUBSCRIBERS NAMES.

A

BOYD Alexander, Efq. of Southbar
Mrs. Alexander, ditto
Mrs. Alexander of Ballamile
Mr. Robert Ainfley, writer, Edinburgh
Mrs Arnot of Dalwhatfwood
Mrs. Auftine, Edinburgh
Mr. Armftrong, Braikwoodlees
Mr. William Armftrong, writer, Langholm
Mr. John Armftrong, Eives
Mr. John Armftrong, Wier
Mr. John Aitchifon, Annan
Mr. John Aitchifon, Newbic
Mr. Thomas Archibald, Ardry
Mr. Francis Allwood, Shuttlefton
Mr. Robert Allan, Catrine
Mr. Andrew Anderfon, Glafgow
Mr. Robert Allafon, ditto
Mr. Agnew, Caftlewig
Robert Anderfon, Efq. of Borland
Mr. William Andrew, Oldhall
Mr. Thomas Aiton, Woodhead
Mr. James Aitken, Cairn
Mr. Alexander Ainfley, Prince' ftreet, Edinburgh
Mr. James Alexander, Union Bank, Paifley
Mr. William Alexander, manufacturer, ditto
Mr. John Andrew of Coldftream
Dr. Adair, Edinburgh
Mifs Adair, ditto

B

HONOURABLE Mr. Boyle, Irvine
Honourable Mrs. Boyle, ditto
Sir John Hunter Blair
T. Boyle, Esq. of Shouilston
Robert Baillie Esq. of Mayvill
Miss Lesly Baillie
Mrs. Baillie of Canal-bank
James Boswell, Esq. of Auchinleck
Richard Bousiher, Esq. Bath
William Blair Esq. of Blair
Mrs. Blair of ditto
Mrs Bushbie, Tinwaldowns, 2 copies
Miss Bushbie
Thomas Beattie Esq. of Cruvie
Alexander Benton Esq. of Lamberton
George James Bell, Esq. advocate, Edinburgh
James Buchannan Esq.
Alexander Brown, Esq.
Mr. A. Blair, writer to the signet, Edinburgh
Mr. David Balfour, writer to the signet, ditto
Rev. Mr. Thomas Brisbane, Dunlop
Mr. Hugh Breckenridge. of Daldarick
Mr. William Bell, Argyle street, Glasgow, 4 copies
Miss Bell, 2 copies
Mr. James Bell, 2 copies
Mr. William Balfour, Glasgow
Mr. Blair, George' street, Edinburgh
Mrs. Balmain, Hill street, ditto
Miss Balmain
Mrs. Buchannan, Sydorf, Hanover street
Mrs. Bell, Queen's street
Mr. James Brown, Loudoun kirk
Mr. James Brown, Fenwick
Mr. John Begbie, Kilmarnock
Miss Bosland, Paisley
Mr. William Brown, writer, Kilmarnock *now*
Mr. James Brown, Blacklaw
Mr. James Brown, merchant, Kilmarnock
Robert Borland, Esq
Mr. William Babington
Miss J. Brown of Waterhause
Miss M. Brown, ditto
Mr. Andrew Brown, writer, Stewarton
Mr John Beg, Cairn

Mr. James Bell, Ecclefechen
Mr. C. Baillie, Matterstain
Mr. David Blackwood, Stewarton
Mr. Robert Baird, Drumkelly
Mr. Richard Beattie, Lochmaben
Mr. Stairs Beck, Charlesfield
Mr. James Beck, Allenby
Mr. John Burle, cotton manufacturer, Annan
Mr. James Burnie, Kilnhead
Mr. David Black, Longbridge
Mr. Patrick Blackstock, Woodside
Mr. John Blacklock, Cummertrees
Mr. David Blair
Mr. Thomas Buchannan, merchant, Glasgow
Mr. James Buchannan, merchant, ditto
Mr. Robert Boyd, do
Mr. John Baird, LIII. Regiment
Mr. James Baird, Niddrie
Mrs Catharine Beattie, Ballamile
Mr. Robert Burns, Dumfries

C

LADY Elizabeth Creichton, 2 copies
Lady Mary Cameron
Sir William Cunningham of Robertland
Miss J. F. Crawford, 2 copies
Mr Cameron
Ronald Crawford, Esq of Frisky
Mrs. Cunningham junior, of Auchenskeith
Peter Clark, Esq. of Holms
Mrs. Clark, ditto
Arthur Campbell, Esq. of Auchmunnoch
Colonel J. W. Crawford of Crawfordland
George Cranston Esq. advocate, Edinburgh
David Cathcart, Esq advocate, ditto
Miss Jane Cathcart
James Campbell, Esq. ditto
John Carse, Esq. of Gardrum
Henrick Cape, Esq. Glasgow
Miss Carr, Edinburgh
Mrs. Craigie, Hay street, Edinburgh
Mrs. Campbell of Netherplace
Mrs. Clark, Standingstone, Cumberland
Willisred Clark, ditto
Ewan Clark, ditto

Mr. James Cathcart, Queen's street, Edinburgh
S. Crawford, Tuland
Mr. Cunningham Corbet, Glafgow
Mr. William Clydefdale, Glafgow
Mr. William Currie, ditto
Mr. John Crofs, ditto
Mr. James Campbell, ditto
Mr. Colin Campbell, ditto
Mr. James Campbell, for D.
Mr. James Carruthers, Moufwald
Mr. William Caldwell of Middleton
Mr. Hume Cranfton, Edinburgh
Mr. John Clark, XXXV. Regiment
Mrs Cunningham, Langfhaw
Mifs Cunningham, Glafgow
Mr. George Chriftie, Paifley, 2 copies
Mifs Chriftie, do.
Mrs. Crofs, Greenlaw, do.
Mrs. Campbell, Waterhaufe
Mr. Thomas Corfan, Druggift, Kilmarnock
Mr. M. Cunningham of Seabank
Mr. Patrick Campbell, writer to the fignet, Edinburgh
Mr. Andrew Cromie,
Mr. David Craig, Dunlop
Mr. William Carlington, Caldweil
Mr. William Cochran, Glanderfton
Mr. Allan Cochrane ·
Mr. Thomas Corfan, Lochryan
Mr. John Carruthers, Brocklihearft
Mr. William Chalmers, bookfeller, Dumfries, 2 copies
Mr. James Clindinning, ditto
Mr. William Cleland, Glafgow
Mrs. Carruthers, Supplebank
Mifs J. Carruthers, Cummertrees
Mr. Charles Ewart, Dalton
Mr. James Corbet
Mr. William Carmichael, Craigie
Mr. Robert Carlyle
Mr. Walter Cook
Mr. John Cathcart, Moffat
Mr. Charles Crawford, Killhead
Mr. James Carruthers
Mr. Walter Cowan, Bygate
Mr. Jardine Combe, Ecclefechan

Mr. Alexander Craig, Dumfries
Mr. George Clapperton, furgeon, Annan
Mr. Thomas Chalmers, Hannah

D

EARL of Dumfries, 2 copies
Countefs of Dumfries, 2 copies
Countefs of Dalhoufie
Right Honourable Lord Dair, St. Mary's Ifle
Lady Ifabella Douglas
Lady Eleonora Dalziel
Lady Douglas of Killhead, 2 copies
Mrs. Dunlop of Dunlop, 7 copies
Major Dunlop, 6 copies
Mifs K. Dunlop, 7 copies
Mifs A. E. Dunlop, 2 copies
George Douglafs, Efq; of Roadenhead, 2 copies
Colonel Alexander Dundafs
Mr. William Dundafs
Mifs Dundafs of Dundafs
James Dewar, Efq; of Vogrie
Captain Dumbar, Douglas
Mr. William Dalziel, writer to the fignet, Edinburgh
David Douglas Efq; advocate
Robert Davidfon, Efq; advocate
Mr. James Donaldfon, fenior, merchant, Glafgow
Mr. David Dale, junior, ditto
Mr. James Donaldfon, junior, ditto
James Duncafter, Efq;
Rev. Mr. Jacob Dickfon, Moufwald
Rev. Mr. David Dickfon, St. Mungo
Rev. Mr. James Dewar, Fenwick
Rev. r. Duncan, Ardroffan
Mr. James Douglas, Loudoun
Mr. Dalziel, Queen ftreet, Edinburgh
Mr. James Duncan, furgeon, ditto
Mifs Davies, Dumfries
Mr. Matthew Dickie of Knockingdale
Mr. Robert Dunlop, Aurthurby
Mr James Dobie, Beith
Mr. John Dun, Loanhead
Mr. James Dunlop of Loanhead
Mr. Thomas Dunlop of Aiket

Mr. Abraham Dickson, Harrington
Mr. Thomas Dickson, Mouswald
Mr. John Dalrymple, Branthat
Mrs. Janet Deens, Hitchel
Mr. Thomas Dickson, Annan
Mr. Robert Dickson, ditto

E

COUNTESS Dowager of Errol
Governor Edmonston, George' street, Edinburgh
William Erskine, Esq. advocate
John Elliot, Esq. of Whitehaugh
Mr. David Ewart, Chancery office, Edinburgh
Mr. James Elliot, M. D.
Mr. J. Elliot of Flat
Mr. Elliot of Dunlie
Mr. John Elliot of Park
Mr William Elliot, George' square, Edinburgh
Mr. James Easton, student of Divinity, Mouswald
Mr. Archibald Edmonston, Edinburgh
Mr. Walter Ewen, merchant, Glasgow

F

COLONEL William Fullarton of Fullarton, 2 copies
Mrs. Fullarton
S. M. Fullarton of Bartonholm
Mr. Fergusson, Beith
Mrs. Fergusson, ditto
Miss H. Fergusson, ditto
James Fergusson Esq. advocate, Edinburgh, 5 copies
Robert Fergusson, Esq. Tennant, 2 copies
John Fletcher, Esq. of Dowings
Mr. John Fergusson, Glasgow
Rev. Mr. James Foster, A. B. English Chapel, Glasgow
Rev. Mr. Peter Fergusson, Inch
Mr. Alexander Fowlds, Kilmarnock
Mr. Foster, Pasterhead
Miss Fisher, Dykemount
Mr. James Fisher, Minive, 2 copies
T. Ferrier, Esq. George' street, Edinburgh
Miss Ferrier, ditto
Mr Archibald Fletcher, ditto
Mr. Robert Flemen, ditto

Mr. Allan Forfyth, ditto
Mr James Fairly, Cairn
Mr. Alexander Ferguffon, Stewarton
Mr. John Forreft, Annan

G

EARL of Glafgow
Countefs of Glafgow
Honourable Francis Grey, 7 copies
General Gordon
Lady Margaret Grierfon, Rochal
George Greenlaw, Efq. of Hilton
John Gordon, Efq. of Carleton
Archibald Grahame, Efq. Glafgow
Alexander Gardiner, writer to the Signet
Dr Robert Glafgow of St Vincents
Rev. Mr. George Gordon, Sorn, 2 copies
Mrs. Gordon, 2 copies
Rev Mr. Greenfield, Edinburgh
Mifs Guthry, Argyle fquare, ditto
Rev. Mr James Grant, Libertone
Mr. James Galloway, writer, Glafgow
Mr. John Geddis, Glafswork, ditto
Mr. James Gregg, writer, Kilmarnock
Mr. Thomas Greenfhields, ditto
Mr. John Greenfhields
Mr. A Gillian, London
Mr. A. Gillies, Edinburgh
Mr. James Gibfon, ditto
Mifs Graham, Dumfries
Mr Archibald Gordon
Mr Robert Grierfon, B. D Edinburgh, 2 copies
Mr. William Grahame, Drumlanrig Caftle, 2 copies
Mifs Charlotte Grant
Mr John Graham Foxhall, Finifton, 2 copies
Mifs Graham, Edinburgh
Mrs Gordon, Greenlaw
Mr George Gregg, Hoddam Caftle
Mr George Grahame, merchant, Langholm
Mr. James Gibfon, Ecclefechan
Mr. John Glover, Hillhead
Mr. Walter Graham, Powfoot
Mr James Gibfon, Caldwell
Mifs J. Gemmel, Dunlop

Mr. William Guthrie, Harperland
Mr. J. Guthrie, Dollars
Mr. William Gordon, Edinburgh
Mr. John Grahame, Paisley
Mr J. Graham, manufacturer, ditto
Mr. Thomas Gemmel, Caldwell
Mr. John Goven, Patterhill

H

EARL of Hume
Earl of Hopeton
Countess of Hopeton, 4 copies
Lady Margaret Hope
Honourable Charles Hope
Lady Charlotte Hay
Lady Isabella Anne Hay
Sir James Hall, Bart. Dunglass
William Hamilton, Esq. Edinburgh
Dr. William Hamilton, Kilmarnock
J. Hunter, Esq. writer to the signet, Edinburgh, 2 copies
Alexander Hamilton, Esq. of Grange
William Hamilton, Esq of Middlepart
Mr Robert Hamilton, Edinburgh
Mr James Hagart, do.
Mr Thomas Hopekirk, do
Mr Francis Howden, do.
Mr James Howden, do
Rev. Mr. James Hall, do. 2 copies
Mr John Hall, teacher, Glasgow, 2 copies
Mr John Hall, writer, do
Rev. Mr. James Headrick, Glasgow
Captain George Hope, R. N.
Ninian Hume Esq. of Paxton
Mrs. Hume of ditto
Patrick Hume Esq. of Wedderburn
Miss Hume, ditto
Miss M. J. Hume
Miss Hume, Broomhouse
James Hume Esq of Newmills
Miss Hume, ditto
George Hume Esq. of Branxton
Mr. James Hume, Edinburgh
George Hardie, Esq. Annan

Miss Hunter of Thurston
Miss S. Hawthorn, Castlewig, Edinburgh
Miss C. Hawthorn, ditto
Mrs. Hawthorn Stewart of Phisgill
Mrs. Henry, Bourdeaux, 8 copies
Mr. James Henderson, Hudliscleugh
Mr. David Hunter, George' street Edinburgh
Mr. Robert Hay, Wellmeadows
Mr. Roger Hall, Stewarton
Miss Hugan, Glasgow
Mr. James Harris, ditto
Mr. Charles Haushet, Candleriggs, ditto
Mrs. Henderson, Camlongan
Miss Henderson, ditto.
Mr. Andrew Hunter
Mr Robert Henderson
Mr. C. Hope, advocate, St. Andrew's square, Edinburgh
Mr. Simon Hall, merchant, Ecclefechan
Mr. John Henry, Surgeon, ditto
Mr Thomas Hetherton, Stonebridge
Mr. John Hill, Winterseugh
Mr. James Henderson, Hightea
Mr. Alex. Harkness, Gotterby

I, J

LADY G. Johnston
Lady Anne Johnston
Lady Jemina Johnston
Lady Lucy Johnston
Miss Johnston, Creichton street, Edinburgh
James Johnston, Esq. of Alva
Mr. James Johnston, Blenereffet
Miss Johnston Killhead
Miss Catharine Johnston, ditto
Mrs Johnston, Charlesfield
Mr. Robert Johnston, Student, Edinburgh
Mr. William Johnston, Glasgow
Mr. J. Johnston, Cummertrees
Mr. Robert Johnston, Kerr
Mr. John Johnston, Winterseugh
Professor Jardine, Glasgow
Mr. John Javan, King street, do,
Mr. Christopher Irvine, do.

Mr. William Irvine, Glasgow
Rev. Mr. Jeffery, Kilmarnock
Mr. John Jeffery, Edinburgh
Mr. Henry Jamieson, Gayfield-place
Mr. David Jackson, Netherrow
Mr. William Inglis, Milnholm
Mr. James Irvine, Milnpath
Mr. Alexander Irvine, Killhead
Mr. Thomas Irvine, Annan

K

REV. Mr. William Kilpatrick, Dumfries
Miss Kincald of Kincald
Miss Kennedy
Mr. James King, Aurthurly
Mr. Thomas Kerr, Moufwald
Mr. George Kyle, Heughead
Miss Kennedy, Antigua street, Edinburgh
Mr. John King, teacher of vocal music

I.

THE Countess of Loudoun, 12 copies
Colonel Laurie, Bath, 6 copies
James Pit Laurie, Esq. Honduras, 3 copies
Rev. Dr. Laurie, Newmilns
Mr. Archibald Laurie, ditto, 2 copies
Miss B. Laurie
Mrs. Lockhart of Carnwath
John Lumsdair, Esq. of Bienem
Rev. Mr. Lauson, Dumfries
Miss C. Lindsay, Burleshall
John Lowes, Esq. Ridgely-hall, Northumberland, 2 copies
Mrs. Laughton, Great Russel street, Bloomsbury, London,
    2 copies
R. Lindsay, Esq. of Bourtreehill, 2 copies
Mr. George Lewis M'Murdo, Broadlee
Mr. Francis Laing, writer, Edinburgh
Mr. David Litster, do.
Mr. William Lyal, Glasgow
Mr. Laing, Paisley
Mr. William Lockhart, Edinburgh
Mr. Robert Lauchlan, Eaglesham
Mr. John Lapraik, Galston

Mr. David Loudoun, Ardry
Mr. John Law, Cumberland
Mr. William Laidlaw, mathematician, Edinburgh
Mr. Stewart Lewis, Ecclefechan
Mr. David Lawson, Halton
Mr. Alexander Lennox
Mr. David Laing, writer, Glasgow
Mr. John Little, writer, Annan
Mr. John Little, Langholm
Mifs Grace Little, do.
Mr. William Little, ilfgate
Mr. Robert Little, Standingftone, 8 copies
Mr. Robert Little, Whifgills
Mr. Robert Little, Whithaugh
Mr. David Little, Branthwat
Mr. John Little, Blough

M

SIR William Maxwell of Springkell, baronet
Lady Maxwell, do.
Lieut. David Maxwell, Broomholm
David Monypenny, Efq. Advocate, Edinburgh
John M'Farquhar, Efq. M. S. Edinburgh.
Robert Morris, Efq of Craig
Hugh Morton, Efq. of Greenbank
James M'Aullay, Efq. Bath, 2 copies
Mifs Maxwell of Polloch
Mifs B. Maxwell, do.
William Muir, Efq. of Caldwell, 7 copies
Mrs. Muir of Warifton, 7 copies
Dr. Moor, London
Mrs. Moor, do.
Mr. George Munro
Mifs E. Munro
Mr James Main, Paifley
Mr. Rofs M'Key
Mr. Charles M'Key, Edinburgh
Mr. William M'Donald, do.
Mr. John Miller, do.
Mr. Wolfe Murray, do.
Mr. William Mole, do.
Mr. James Moubray, do.
Rev. Mr. Thomas Martin, Langholm
B

Rev. Mr. James M'Millan, Torthorwald
Mr. William M'Farlane
Mr. T. M'Carter, Dr. Jeffery's College, Glasgow
Mr. Robert Montgomery of Bogston
Mr. William M'Nish, postmaster, Stranraer, 2 copies
Mr. James M'Gown, surgeon Stow
Lieut. Alexander M'Donald, Rodenhead
Mrs. J. Mitchell, Friendlesshead
Mr. J. Muir, merchant Kilmarnock
Miss A. M'Laughlan, Paisley
Mr. Thomas M'Culloch, Croach
Mr. J. M'Key, Stranraer
Rev. Mr. J. M'Kenzie Port Patrick
Mr. P. M'Dowal, Cairn
Mr. M'Whirter, do
Mr. John Morton, Loudoun Castle
Mr James Mason, Loudoun Kirk
Mr. George M'Gill, Kilmaurs
Mr. Thomas Muir, Milsgate
Mrs. M'Gill of Kingsingcleuch
Mr John M'Kenzie, surgeon, Mauchline
Mr. Matthew Morrison, do
Mr. William M'Dowal, Glasgow
Mr. James M'Nair, writer, do.
Peter Murdoch, Esq.
Mrs. Jane Marshal, Cockbridge
Mr. Hugh Maxwell, Dumfries
Miss Malcom, Westerkirk
Mr. James Moffat, surgeon, Langholm
Mr. Thomas Murray, Whisgills
Mr. James M'Kie, Gatterbie
Mr. John Miller, Clayhouse
Mr. James Moffat, Hightea
Miss Eliza M'Claren, Kilhead
Mr. Matthew Murray, merchant, Langholm
Mr. James Moffat, Ecclefechan
Mr. William M'Nae, Sandbed
Miss M'Cleod, George' street, Edinburgh
Mrs. M'Kie, Hanover street, do.
Mr. George M'Intosh, Glasgow, 4 copies
Mrs. M'Intosh, do. 2 copies
Mr. Charles M'Intosh
Miss F. M'Intosh
Miss Polson M'Intosh

Mr. John M'Intosh
Mr. Andrew M'Intosh
Mr. John M'Clean, surgeon, Glasgow
Mr. James M'Clatchie, Dumfries
Mr. William M'Dowall, Buchannan street, Glasgow
Mr John M'Naught, do.
Mr Francis Murray, Trongate, do.
Mr John Milligan, do.
Mr. William Mitchell
Mr William Millar, Glasgow
Mr. Samuel M'Caul, do
Mr. Andrew Macaulay, bookseller, do. 12 copies

N

HONOURABLE Miss Napier, Prince' street, Edinburgh
Archibald Nisbet Esq. of Sornhill
James Napier, Esq. Edinburgh
Michael Nicholson Stewart, Esq. of Carnock
Mrs. Nicholson, do.
Mr. Andrew Nixon, Langholm
Mr. Thomas Nixon, Blinkbonny
Mr. Neilson
Miss S. Nicholis, Edinburgh

O

MRS. Ogilvie of Broomlie
Alexander Osburn, Esq Customhouse
Miss Orde, George' street, Edinburgh
Miss Eliza Orde, do.
Mr. J. Owen, schoolmaster, Cummertrees
Mr. Robert Orr, Paisley

P

WILLIAM PARKER, Esq. of Corraith
Mr. Parichon, London, 2 copies
Professor Playfair, Edinburgh
Captain Archibald Paton, Glasgow
Mr. Robert Purdon, do.
Mr. Paisley, teacher, Carlisle
Mr. Andrew Pollock, A. Houstin's, Glasgow
Mr. Alexander Pearson, Hanover street, Glasgow
Mr. J. Parker, junior, Kilmarnock

Miss Paton, Neilston
Mr. J. Paton, Clearmount
Mr. P. Philips, Ruthwell
Miss Paterson, Gill
Mr. David Porteous, Oldmiln
Mr. Andrew Pickens, Shuttleston

R

DOCTOR Rutherford, Edinburgh
John Richardson, Esq. of Bufs, 2 copies
William Rae, Esq. advocate, Edinburgh
Miss Sophia Richardson, Stank
Mr. Thomas Rynd, Union Bank, Paisley
James Ramsay, Esq.
Mr. William Riddle, Glasgow
Mr. Stephen Rowan, do.
Mr. Alexander Rough, Ballamile
Mr. John Rankine, Boghead
Mr. John Rankine, Caldwell
Mr. John Robertson, do.
Mr. . Richmond, Loudoun-kirk
Mr. William Roxburgh, Finwick
Mr. James Renie, Trongate, Glasgow
Mr. Reid of Adamton
Mr. Alexander Ramsay, Glasgow
Miss P. Richardson
Mr. James Rome, Ruthwell
Mr. James Rae, Killhead
Mr. William Rodgerson, Dumfries
Rev. Mr. Reid, Mauchline

S

SIR J. Sinclair of Ulster
Lady S. Sinclair
Charles Sharp Esq. of Hodam
Mrs. Sharp, do.
Miss Sharp, do.
William Stewart, Esq. of Hillside
Mrs. Charles Stewart, Monteith, Closeburnhall, 2 copies
James Stewart, Esq. of Stewart-hall
John Shaw Stewart, Esq. of Greenock, 2 copies
Mrs. Shaw Stewart, do.

Miss Secombe
Dr. Smith, physician, Bath
John Scott, Esq. of Hopesridge
Miss Scott of Ancrum
Mrs. Stewart, Argyle street, Edinburgh, 2 copies
John Swanson, Esq. Glasgow
John Stark, Esq. do.
Mr James Steven, junior, do.
Rev. Mr. Steven, Catrine
Rev Mr Smith, Cummertrees
Rev. Mr. Smith, Galston
Mr. Robert peed, Edinburgh
Mr. John Swinton, ditto
Mr. Archibald Swinton
Mr. William Staig
Miss Stevens, Edinburgh
Mrs. Scott, Forge, Cannonby
Mr David Scott, banker, Air
Mr. Adam Smiats, Westburn Fla
Miss Stewart, Ashton, Edinburgh
Mr. Charles Shaw, writer, Air
Miss Somervile, Kenox
Mr. E. Sheriff, Paisley
Mr. Stewart, do.
Mr. Slaiter, do.
Mr. James Spence, Edinburgh
Mr. Robert Spear, Templeton
Mr. James Smail, Caldwell
Mr. James Smith, Newmilns
Mr. James Senier, Glasgow
Mr Thomas Stevens, Whitby
Mr. Alex. Scott, Glasgow
Mr Thomas Scott, Langholm
Mr. Francis Smith, Catrine
Mr. Peter Stewart, do.
Mr. Thomas Scott, Craiglockhart
Mr. Moses Steven, merchant, Glasgow
Mr. James Steel, Alton
Mr John Smith, Dunlop
Miss Sked, Hundh

T

FRANCIS TYTLER, advocate, Edinburgh
Mr. Todd, Dean street, London

Mrs Todd, Dean ftreet, London
Mr. James Thomfon, ftudent of divinity, Kilmarnock
Mrs. Trotter of Mortonhall, 4 copies
Mr. William Thomfon, teacher, Carlifle
Mr. J. Torrance. Catrine
Mr. James Turnbull, Edinburgh
Mr. George Turner, Bolton gate
Mr. James Thomfon, Cummertrees
Mr. Robert Turner, Ardry
Mrs. Trotter, Glafgow

W

SIR John Wedderburn, Ballendean
Dr. Walker, Edinburgh
Mr. J. Wilfon, junior, Glafgow
Mr. James Wyllie, do.
Mr. Williamfon, Edinburgh
Mr. A Wachop, fenior, Niddry, 3 copies
Mr. A. Wachop, junior, do. 3 copies
Mifs M. Wachop, do. 2 copies
Mifs Alice Wachop, do
Mr. Robert Wight, Kingfknow
Mr Robert Wood
Capt. Wallace of Cairnhill
Mrs. Warner, Irvine
Mr. Alexander Walker, Air
Mr. Samuel Watfon, Edinburgh
Mr. David Williamfon, do.
Mrs. Watfon, Abbotfinch
Mr. Wallace, Queen ftreet, Edinburgh
Mr Alexander Williamfon, Giafgow
Mr. J. Woodburn Shawmiln
Mr. Alexander Wilfon, Paifley
Mr. Thomas Wilfon, Stewarton
Mr J Wightman Cummertrees
Mrs Walker, Smailholm, 2 copies
Mr Weir, furgeon, Edinburgh
Mr. William Wilfon, Birmingham
Mr. T. Wood, Whitehall
Mr. Dan Wilkinfon
Mr. John Wilkinfon
J Wilfon, bookfeller, Kilmarnock
P. Wilfon

V

Mr Vance Agnew, 3 copies
Mrs. Vance Agnew, 4 copies

Y

Charles Young, Fsq. Edinburgh
Rev. Mr. James Yorkston, Hoddam
Mr. J. Young, merchant, Glasgow
Mr. William Yates, Ardry
Mr. William Young, Shuttleston
Mr. William Yeoman

ERRATA.

P. 44 l. 8. from the head, *for* nor, *read* or.
P. 46. line 8 from the head, *for* delusive, *read* decisive.
P. 51. laſt line, *for* Golanda, *read* Golconda.
P 54. line 2. from the head, *for* my, *read* buy.
P. 69 line 7. from the head, *for* nor, *read* no.
P. 81. line 5. from the head, *for* expanded, *read* extended.
P. 90. line 9. from the head, *for* Claudia, *read* Claudius.
P 139 line 9. from the head, *for* the, *read* his.
P. 159. line 4. *for* of, *read* or.
P. 170. line 8. *for* game, *read* dance.

WILL gentle LOUDOUN deign to lend
      an ear,
When nature fpeaks, and forrow drops a tear?
Within your walls my happinefs I found
Luxuriant flourifh, like the plants around :
Blithe as the birds that perch on yonder fpray,
In joyous notes, I pour'd the willing lay.
Beneath your roof thefe humble lines had
      birth,
Whofe honour'd Patrons now lie low in earth;

Or borne by Fate far from their native ſhore,
With ſmiles auſpicious glad my heart no
 more.

 Here youth and beauty, innocence and
 love,
I joy'd to ſee, to ſerve, and to approve:
Here honour'd Age to all around did ſhow,
That virtue's paths alone can bliſs beſtow:
Here moral leſſons ſpoke from ev'ry part,
And peace and kindneſs wrote them on my
 heart.
Hoary inhabitants around the place,
Whoſe faithful ſervices obtain'd that grace,
'Mid ev'ry comfort rural life affords,
Shower prayers and bleſſings on its former
 Lords.

 To you the young are taught to lift the eye,
Mild morning ſun of their unclouded ſky.
Bleſt in a lot left nothing to deſire,
Thoſe happy ſcenes did future hopes inſpire,
That thus my life in careleſs eaſe might run,
My age ſupported by my maſter's ſon;

In him, that goodnefs, and thofe virtues find,
Which grateful numbers meet in you combin'd.

Ah! like a changeful vifion of the night,
Thofe fcenes are fled, and death appals my
  fight!
Where'er I turn, lamented tombs appear,
Or parting fails extort the bitter tear!
To diftant realms the darling child too gone;
O guard him heav'n, and let me weep alone!
For ev'ry tear, let countlefs bleffings fall
On thy fad mother in thy grandfire's hall!

Forgive, fair nymph, the dictates of defpair;
Grief flies, for comfort, to the tender fair.
The good and great, we fondly think have
  pow'rs,
Can charm to eafe our fad and anxious hours;
Elfe why to you fhould I at Fate repine?
The friends I mourn, alas! were *doubly* thine!

For their dear fakes, bid lines they priz'd
      ftill live,
And grant that fhelter they no more can give.
Yet, the fad verfe how fhould you patronize
That wakes up anguifh in a heart at eafe!
For their dear fakes my pray'rs are ever
      thine,
Nor can I more were your protection mine.

THE PUBLIC.

———————

I.

FROM the dull confines of a country
      shade,
A ruftic damfel iffues forth her lays;
There fhe, in fecret, fought the Mufe's aid,
    But now, afpiring, hopes to gain the bays.

II.

" Vain are her hopes," the fnarling critic cries;
   " Rude and imperfect is her rural fong."

C

But fhe on public candour firm relies,
    And humbly begs they'll pardon what is
    wrong.

III.

And if fome lucky thought, while you perufe,
    Some little beauty ftrike th' inquiring
    mind;
In gratitude fhe'll thank th' indulgent Mufe,
    Nor count her toil, where you can pleafure
    find.

IV.

Upon your voice depends her fhare of fame,
    With beating breaft her lines abroad are
    fent:
Of praife fhe'll no luxuriant portion claim;
    Give but a little, and fhe'll reft content.

P O E M S.

T O

H O P E.

I.

HAIL meek-ey'd maid! of matchlefs
worth!
Our beft companion here on earth;
   To thee fole pow'r is giv'n,
T' illume our dark and dreary way,
As through life's mazy path we ftray,
   And bend our fteps to heav'n.
'Tis thine to fmooth the rugged vale,
   To ftem the trickling tear;

Thy whifpers, as the fpicy gale,
　　Do drooping trav'llers cheer.
　　　　Incline thou, to fhine now
　　　　　Upon me as I go;
　　　　　Thy favour fhall ever
　　　　　Alleviate my wo.

IL.

Thy prefence calms the raging feas,
And to the throbbing breaft gives eafe
　　Amid the tempeft's howl,
When waves appear as mountains high,
When fwelling furges dafh the fky,
　　And foaming billows roll;
When danger, with uplifted hand,
　　Proclaims th' approaching doom,
Thou gently doft the ftroke withftand,
　　And diffipates the gloom.
　　　　When caring, defpairing,
　　　　　And deeming all as loft,
　　　　Thy rays will portray ftill
　　　　　The long expected coaft.

III.

Thou animates the hero's flame ;
To him prefents a deathlefs name
   In the enfanguin'd field :
Thou doft his nerves with valour brace,
Bids him, with bold undaunted face,
   Deftructive weapons wield.
War's trumpet, breathing rude alarms,
   Strikes terror all around ;
Thy voice of fame, and honour's charms,
   Outvies the direful found.
     When falling, appalling
       The tumults wild increafe,
     On wings then, thou brings then
       The harbinger of peace.

IV.

Thy power elates the ftudent's views ;
The paths of fcience kindly ftrews
   With never-fading flow'rs.
Depriv'd of thee, how lovers mourn

Dejected, reftlefs and forlorn,
 In unfrequented bow'rs!
Attending ftill on Hymen's rites,
 Thou decorates the chain;
Thy fmile the fprightly maid invites
 And lures the youthful fwain:
  Still eafing, and pleafing,
   When ftern misfortune ftares,
  'Mid loffes, and croffes,
   Thou lightens all their cares.

V.

From life's fair dawn to liart eve,
We all thy flatt'ring tales believe,
 Enamour'd of thy art:
Thy foft and falutary voice
Gives birth to unexpected joys,
 And foothes the bleeding heart:
And even at our lateft hour,
 When earthly comforts fly,
Thou doft, by a fuperior Pow'r,
 Death's terrors all defy.

Not grieving, when leaving
   This fcene of dole and care,
But viewing, purfuing
   A more exalted fphere.

HAPPINESS.

O HAPPINESS! where art thou to be
found ?
What bow'r is bleſt with thy perpetual gleam?
From court, from cot, ev'n while they ſeek
thy ſtay,
On thy ſoft pinions, rapid is thy flight.
Thy name, not ſubſtance, is to mortals
known.

Repulſe from thee makes drunkards ſtand
aghaſt,
Who nightly revel o'er the flowing bowl.
In vain they ſeek thy progreſs to retard,
A gueſt too noble to be thus detain'd.

Thy quick elopement shews their sad mistake;
Baulks hope, and certain disappointment
  brings.

Misers for thee grope 'midst their bags
  of wealth,
Nor find thy residence in golden ore:
Fear, anxious care, bleak av'rice, and distrust,
Forbid thy access to the grov'ling soul.

Not riches, though in gorgeous pomp ar-
  ray'd,
With all the dazzling splendour of the east,
Secure thee 'mongst the gay, fantastic train.
Pride and Ambition, vulture-like, appear,
G'in access to the op'lent master's heart,
And bid defiance to thy sacred charms,
Now swiftly banish'd from his sumpt'ous
  seat.

Nor even the voice of honour can recal
Thy hasty steps: thee Pleasure sues in vain;
A stranger to the gay, licentious crowd,

The giddy flutt'ring fons of dance and fong.
Thou to the libertine doft ever prove
An airy phantom; mock'ft his eager grafp;
Leaves him to cruel difappointment's rage,
Remorfe, defpair, the inmates of his foul.

In hopes to meet thee in fome diftant
    clime,
The ardent warrior quits his native fhore,
Inur'd to martial toil; at danger fmiles,
And unconcern'd treads o'er the heaps of
    flain:
His en'mies fly before him; at his feet
Millions fall proftrate, and for mercy call:
Yet ftill in vain he makes his court to thee;
Thou fcarce vouchfafes him one aufpicious
    fmile.

See lovers too, in yon fequefter'd grove,
Seek lonely walks, and fpend their fighs in
    vain,
For thee! For what? for fome bewitching
    fair,

Whofe fmiles they deem can boundlefs blifs
    fecure:
Their views contracted would thee thus con-
    fine.

Nor art thou found in Hymen's facred
    rites,
Though filken cords of fweet affection bind.
A thoufand ills encompafs the fond pair,
And mix their fweets with bitternefs and wo.
Bent in purfuit, through many a devious
    track,
All feem to fay, "Succefslefs is the fearch;
To nobler objects henceforth bend your view."

All hail, Religion! thou celeftial power!
Thy force alone can foothe the anxious breaft,
And quite difpel the folitary gloom,
Thefe fullen fhades that fteal upon the foul.
O let me hear thy falutary voice!
Thy facred dictates let me ftill revere;
And ever prone in virtue's fteps to tread,
My hopes, my wifhes center'd all in' Him,
Whofe hand omnipotent the world did frame.

O Thou, great Source of all fupreme de-
　　light!
Without reluctance may I ever prove
Submiffive to thy providential fway,
To know and to obferve thy laws divine,
My fole folicitude.
How mean foe'er my humble ftation be,
Content, and calm ferenity of mind,
Shall pave my paths along the rugged vale;
And when the vain delufive vifion's paft,
Then happinefs, in all its vaft extent
Unmeafurable, ignorant of bounds,
Shall through eternal ages be my lot;
The lot of all whofe hope is fix'd on thee.

LOUDOUN CASTLE.

WHAT means this silent, solitary
          gloom?
All nature in her difhabille appears;
Contracted flow'rets yield no fweet perfume,
And ev'ry grove a difmal afpect wears.

Nor do the joys of Autumn glad our plains;
Our landfcapes are in fable weeds array'd;
No jocund found is heard among the fwains,
And nought but fighs from each dejected
        maid.

Rude Eurus echoing through the diftant
    woods,
With harfh, difcordant note, augments our
    wo;
While rains, impetuous, from the burfting
    clouds,
Our verdant walks and pleafure-grounds
    o'erflow.

Incumber'd by their foliage now, the trees,
With leaves, untimely dropp'd, beftrew the
    ground :
Becaufe Matilda's prefence does not pleafe,
All bleak and difmal feem the fields around.

Her placid looks befpoke a mind ferene,
Each feature wore an unaffected fmile;
Her's was the pow'r to beautify the fcene,
And fweetly gay the languid hours beguile.

Her count'nance milder than an April morn,
When Phœbus firft emits his infant rays;
More radiant beauties do her mind adorn,
Than ere were brighten'd by his noon-tide
    blaze.

Fair Virtue, cloth'd in all it's native fweets,
Celeftial precepts in her breaft inlaid;
And oft, as friendly intercourfe invites,
In fofteft accents from her lips convey'd.

But now fhe's gone, a fullen fadnefs reigns!
Abforb'd in grief we ftill her abfence mourn,
Or beg that heaven would fmile upon our
   plains,
And grant a bleffing in her fwift return.

☙❧☙❧☙❧☙❧☙❧☙❧☙❧☙❧☙

THE

FICKLE PAIR.

DAMON and Phillis, 'tother day,
 To Hymen's altar haften'd;
They talk'd of love along the way,
 And wifh'd the knot well faften'd.

A church the willing pair perceiv'd,
 With portals wide expanded;
The prieft a fpeedy audience crav'd,
 And in the bride was handed.

When lo! a tremor feiz'd the fair,
 In marriage robes adorned;
She left the youth perplex'd with care,
 The rites yet unperformed.

With eager steps he swift purfu'd
  The object of his wishes,
And with redoubl'd ardour woo'd
  Her to complete his bliss.

The maid, reluctant, turn'd again,
  Some glances kind bestowing;
And well resolv'd appear'd the swain,
  Though with resentment glowing.

Kind Hymen heav'd his torch, while they
  Re-enter'd both together;
But Cupid slily took his way,
  And went—they knew not whither.

The bridegroom next—but what of that,
  No bride his absence mourned;
He play'd his charmer tit for tat;
  He went but ne'er returned.

Philander kindly fill'd his place;
  To Damon Chloe consented.
That night they wed, O woful case!
  And ere next morn repented.

D

TO

A LADY,

A PATRONESS OF THE MUSES,

ON HER

RECOVERY FROM SICKNESS.

WHILE ficknefs, madam, on your
      vitals prey'd,
The fympathetic fifters fhar'd your pain:
I mark'd them then in fable weeds array'd,
In concert fad affume the plaintive ftrain.

From Elly's * Land was heard the harp of wo;
A fhepherd, once the blitheft of the throng,
Did mirth infpiring, fportive notes forego,
And fteep'd in tears the melancholy fong.

* The Refidence of the celebrated Poet, Robert Burns.

From *Irvine's* verdant banks, a doleful lay
Re-echo'd .through the groves and diftant
   dale;
Each vocal throat was fill'd with dire difmay,
And heart-felt fighs proclaim'd th' unwel-
   come tale.

Quick and unftable are the turns of Fate;
'Twixt weil and wo are thin partitions rear'd:
I mark'd the drooping choir with hearts elate,
Exulting o'er the ills fo lately fear'd.

When brooding on the verge of deep defpair,
A gladd'ning voice did through the groves
   refound;
Loud acclamations fill'd the ambient air,
And joy and pleafure triumph'd all around.

Health, blooming goddefs, re-affum'd her
   fway,
And did the tender, captive frame releafe;
All feem'd intent the tidings to convey,
In notes more grateful than the whifp'ring
   breeze.

Some greet a patronefs, all hail a friend,
Whofe bofom feels feraphic virtues glow;
Nor further, madam, do your fmiles extend;
Vice dreads your frown, and fhuns you as a
    foe.

Long may you live admir'd by all, and lov'd,
The honour of a long illuftrious race;
Your worth innate, by Envy's felf approv'd,
Which time nor ficknefs never can efface.

CELIA, fair, beyond defcription,
    Soon became the fav'rite toaft;
Charms unrival'd ev'n by fiction,
    Did the lovely maiden boaft.

Beaux and fages, panting, dying,
    Did of love and her complain,
While the nymph, his darts defying,
    Triumph'd o'er her thoufands flain.

With their woes too rafhly fporting,
    Still more fatal darts were fought ;
Anxious to augment her fortune,
    She a lott'ry-ticket bought.

D 3

But old Plutus, fullen power,
    Can the fair and brave withftand;
He, in the delufive hour,
    Shov'd a blank to Celia's hand:

While Brunetta, fhort of ftature,
    Limbs diftorted, fhoulders round,
Gain'd new charms, in fpite of Nature,
    By good thirty thoufand pound.

Celia now, with looks dejected,
    Seem'd the erring wheel to blame,
When the god, with brows erected,
    Did a moment's audience claim.

Go bright Celia, fair and cruel,
    Still of countlefs charms fecure,
Would you heedlefs add more fuel
    To the flames you will not cure?

View the maid to grief inclined,
    Though fhe grafps the golden prize,
O how gladly fhe'd refign it,
    For the conquefts of your eyes!

MONTH'S LOVE.

YE maidens attend to my tale,
  Of love that fly archer take care;
His darts o'er all ranks do prevail,
  The wealthy, the wife, and the fair.

When once his fierce arrow he throws,
  Contentment will bid you adieu;
No potion the doctor beftows,
  Can then be of fervice to you.

Experience prompts me to tell,
  I felt his tyrannical fway;
The time I remember too well;
  It was a long month and a day.

D 4

The youth, I'll not mention his name,
   Who was the sole cause of my smart,
His deeds were unnotic'd by fame,
   His manners unpolish'd by art.

His person could boast of no charm,
   His words of no conquering power;
Yet his footsteps did give the alarm,
   Which made my heart beat for an hour.

When absent from him I ador'd,
   One minute as ages did prove;
Though plenty replenish'd my board,
   I fasted and feasted on love.

My couch but augmented my pain;
   No sleep ever clos'd my eyes;
One glance of my rustic young swain
   Was what I more highly did prize.

None ever bemoan'd my sad case;
   They laugh'd at the ills I endur'd;
But time did my sorrows efface,
   And spite of the imp I was cur'd.

I saw my lov'd youth in the shade,
 Soft whisp'ring to Susan apart;
Resentment came quick to my aid,
 And I banish'd him quite from my heart.

But be not too forward, ye fair,
 Nor take too much courage from me,
How many have fall'n in the snare
 That got not so easily free?

DAMON.

THE fun with keennefs darts his fultry
    ray;
To fome cool fhade Philander hafte away,
Nigh yon finooth riv'let, where the fouthern
    breeze
So foftly plays among the bord'ring trees.
Beneath yon fpreading elm let's reft a while,
And with our fongs the tedious hours beguile:
There will I tune my pipe to Delia's praife,
While ev'ry fwain's attentive to my lays.

PHILANDER.

O Damon! how infipid is thy theme?
Philander's fick of thy lov'd Delia's name:
Nor can the faireft nymph enflave my heart;
Man's foul was form'd to act a nobler part.

This gewgaw train can ne'er my thoughts
    employ ;
Such would difpel but can't augment my joy.
I'll fing the beauties of the breathing fpring,
The treafures Autumn to my barns will
    bring.
To notes of tranfport ever tune my reed,
While on the plains my num'rous flocks I
    feed.

DAMON.

Let Damon's breaft fuch trivial joys difdain ;
What though my flocks o'erfpread the wide
    domain ?
What though my barns were with abun-
    dance ftor'd,
And gen'rous nectar ever grac'd my board ?
Nor honour, riches, though their force unite,
In Delia's abfence ever can delight.
O Delia ! fweeter than the op'ning dawn,
More bright than rays that cheer the dewy
    lawn.
Her fparkling eye the orient gem outfhines,
Or brighteft luftre of Golanda's mines :

Her cheeks of roseate hue, her flaxen hair,
In easy curls, waves gently in the air.
Her coral lips ambrosial sweets retain;
She rivals Juno in her air and mien;
She far exceeds what ancient painters drew,
When fancy's flights the Cyprian queen
        pursue.
Such excellence might grace a prince's arms;
Yet this must yield to her interior charms.
In her fair bosom virtue bears the sway;
There wisdom sheds a pure unmingl'd ray.'
Truth, innocence, and modesty combine
T' adorn her mind, where all perfections
        shine:
Apollo's wit does to the maid belong;
Her voice more charming than the Syren's
        song.

PHILANDER.

Hold, hold, dear Damon, sure too much is said;
Your Delia's then a most bewitching maid:
As blind men judge of colours, so you trace
The matchless beauties of her charming face,

Recount her virtues, and, with partial eyes,
Admire in her what others would defpife.
A fad delirium fure has feiz'd thy brain,
Which makes thee fancy what the poets
    feign,
Of love, and fuch like va'n fantaftic whims,
'Tis wild chimera all, and idle dreams.

DAMON.

And doft thou doubt of fuch a thing as love?
If once thy breaft, like mine, the fmart
    fhould prove,
More than is painted by the poet's art,
In genuine colours will affect thy heart.
But wherefore now contemn my rural lays?
Thy notes were fwell'd once with Lucretia's
    praife!
Does fhe thy favours treat with difrefpect,
Which makes thee now all other maids ne-
    glect!

PHILANDER.

Lucretia ftill appears in all her charms,
A match moft fitting for Philander's arms.

What she posseses yields most solid joy,
Since bags of wealth my pleasures ne'er can
     cloy.
These beauties catch; they set my heart on
     fire;   ·   \
Her farm, her flocks, are all I do admire:
Her darts are powerful, of a yellowish hue,
More fierce than those the fam'd Alcides
     threw.
Her striking beauty in full bloom appears,
At the dull period of full fifty years:
Then Delia will no admiration claim,
But dear Lucretia ever is the same.

DAMON.

For this you love her; now I truly find,
That none but gilded cords your heart can
     bind;
Nor wit nor beauty can obtain your vow;
At Mammon's shrine you still devoutly bow.

PHILANDER.

Vain would th' attempts of either be to hold
My am'rous heart, without the force of gold:

Beauty an empty trifle ftill I deem,

A childifh toy, unworthy of efteem.

Its gaudy foliage may attract the eye;

But as the tulip it will fade and die:

The glowing cheek enamour'd fops may prize,

But men of fenfe can ruby lips defpife.

And what is wit? a giddy flutt'ring thing,

Which can no real fatisfaction bring.

A thoufand ills attend his wretched life,

Whofe dear companion is a witty wife:

Still fhe is right, and ever in the wrong,

Such elocution dwells upon her tongue.

But if affifted by the Mufe's fkill,

He fure may dread the poifon of her quill;

She with keen fatire lafhes all around,

And with the reft her hufband feels the
         wound.

Should poverty, by fudden threats alarm,

Can wit with all its power now prove a charm?

The faireft flowers Parnaffus ere could boaft,

Yield to the treafures of the golden coaft.

The maid who comes fraught with that pre-
         cious ore,

Brings virtue, wit, and beauty all in ftore;

This gives the palid cheek a crimfon glow,
The tawny fkin the tincture of the fnow.
This makes the dwarf complete in ev'ry part:
She wounds moft fure who throws the gol-
    den dart.
Short of one foot, diftorted of one eye,
Struck by its luftre, no defects I fpy.

DAMON.

Thus does Philander wafte his wits to prove
A happy marriage deftitute of love:
Gold, cui fed gold, the bane of ev'ry blifs,
Thy *fummum bonum*, all thy happinefs.
Say, to what purpofe do thy words avail?
Beauty and wit to give us joy may fail.
Wit ceafe to pleafe, and beauty may decay,
Riches make wings and fwiftly fly away;
Depriv'd of all, what will Philander fay?
But to fecure thee of thy darling's charms,
Go to the mines, and lodge within her arms;
Enfold thy miftrefs in a fond embrace,
For ever banifh'd from the fhepherd race.

Nor quit thy manſion till thou breathe thy
    laſt :
Such ſordid ſouls no ſocial joys ſhould taſte.
Bleſt with my Delia on this happy plain,
Where peace and pleaſure in perfection reign,
I'll more ſerenely paſs life's hours away,
Than without her, though crown'd with
    princely ſway.
To pleaſe my charmer all my care ſhall be;
Can I be wretched when ſhe ſmiles on me?
But we muſt go, our fleecy charge attend.
Farewell, Philander, I am ſtill thy friend.
The maid whoſe real charms the heart can
    hold,
Muſt not be deem'd one whit the worſe for
    gold.

NOW from before Aurora's rays,
  Stern darkneſs with its horror flies;
The mountain tops begin to blaze,
  And Phœbus gilds the eaſtern ſkies.

See gliſt'ning dew drops on the buſh,
  Reviving odours cheer the morn;
The warbling blackbird and the thruſh,
  Make vocal ev'ry blooming thorn.

Alexis join the rural lay,
  Give welcome to the op'ning ſpring.
Why figh'ſt thou thus thy hours away?
  Come take thy pipe, and ſoftly ſing.

ALEXIS.

Beneath thefe ivy mantled trees,
    Allow me, Colin, to complain.
No murm'ring brook, nor whifp'ring breeze
    Can in the leaft divert my pain.

The maid, whofe charms I oft have fung,
    Has left the plain, 'twas what I fear'd,
And o'er her fhoulders, carelefs hung,
    A Caledonian plaid appear'd.

Of ancient note on Scotia's plain,
    And by her grandam often wore,
Its crimfon hue was free from ftain,
    Which made Califta fhine the more.

Yea ftill fhe fhines; her radient eyes
    Add luftre to the brighteft day;
Each feature ftrikes with new furprife,
    And various beauties ftill difplay.

But why fhould I recount them ftill?
   'Tis only to increafe my pain.
She bids thefe verdant fields farewell,
   And goes to feek a richer fwain.

Califta, with thy rapid flight,
   Is vanifh'd each delightful gleam.
Can Drife's fair banks give more delight,
   Than Eckles' gently winding ftream?

Do fweeter fcents perfume the grove,
   Or fairer flow'rs adorn the vale?
Do comelier fwains now talk of love,
   And cheer thee with their am'rous tale?

More fprightly youths may feel the fmart,
   And court thee with affiduous care;
But none of all who feek thy heart
   Avows a paffion more fincere.

Then hafte Califta, fave the fwain,
   Who in thy abfence ever fighs;
Add frefher beauties to the plain,
   And bid more pleafing profpects rife.

Give to the flowers a livelier hue;
  Thy prefence makes all nature gay.
O lovely maid! when bleft with you,
  ,Each feafon feems the month of May.

The warblers now, with plaintive note,
  Seem to accord with ev'ry figh;
The fhepherds have their fongs forgot,
  And laid their pipes in filence by.

Since thy retreat, O charming fair!
  Day after day my hopes deftroy.
O fave Alexis from defpair,
  And crown fucceeding fcenes with joy.

FLAVIA.

WHILE dufky fhades eclipfe the folar
　　　ray,
And fanning zephyrs 'mong the branches
　　　play,
Where varied beauties deck the verdant
　　　groves,
Let us recount the ftory of our loves.
Say, dear Almeda, why this penfive mood,
Which does thy wonted cheerfulnefs exclude?

ALMEDA.

The caufe of this to Flavia I'il reveal:
It is a youth whofe power I can't conceal.
'Tis Strephon, who long fince obtain'd my
　　　heart,
When artful Cupid gave the killing dart.

When Strephon's near, no anxious cares mo-
    left,
Nor accefs find to my enraptur'd breaft;
But when he's gone, his abfence ftill I mourn,
And fpend my hours in fighs till he return.

FLAVIA.

You kindle into rapture at his name;
Be wife in time, and guard againft a flame,
Which cherifh'd, hopelefs, will your charms
    efface,
And rob your features of each blooming
    grace.
The dear Caftalia taught my heart to prove
The foft'ning charms and pleafing art of
    love.
Witnefs ye rural walks and verdant vales,
How charm'd I've liften'd to his melting
    tales;
While he, unfkill'd in flatt'ry, did impart,
In flowing ftrains, the dictates of his heart.
Blind was my paffion, long it bore the fway,
Supprefs'd at laft by the enliv'ning ray

E 4

Of Reafon wak'd, by fome celeftial pow'r,
To my relief, in an aufpicious hour,
With open'd eyes I did the charmer view;
Deaf to his accents, from his prefence flew.
Obferve, my precepts are with prudence
    fraught,
What heart fo ftubborn would remain un-
    taught?

ALMEDA.

Command the briny waves no more to flow,
Bid fouthern breezes ever ceafe to blow;
Say to the flowers, no more your fragrance
    yield,
Nor Ceres crown with joy the fertile field;
Bid Phœbus ceafe to gild the op'ning morn,
And Cynthia be of all her beauty fhorn:
Would thefe obedient as thy vaffals prove?
No more can I, dear Flavia, ceafe to love.
A youth poffefs'd of ev'ry moving art,
Quick accefs gains to the fecureft heart.
When he appears, to cheer the drooping plain,
Each nymph enamour'd fpends her fighs in
    vain:

And when in softest strains he tunes his lay,
Each shepherd, envious, throws his lute away.
In him all radiant virtues are combin'd,
True greatness centers in a humble mind;
Truth, candour, justice, in his gen'rous
   breast,
Firm fortitude and soft compassion rest.
Nor can the gods on mortals more bestow,
A bright example of their works below.
Young Strephon's charms, no tongue could
   e'er express;
I may be silent, but can't love him less.

FLAVIA.

Enough is said, Almeda dear, to prove
No fault is seen in those we truly love.
The son of Venus, by a magic art,
Deceives the sight, soon as he wounds the
   heart.
Blind as himself does all his vot'ries make,
Extremely happy in their own mistake.
In all his charms I have young Strephon seen,
Yet never by the youth have wounded been.

Yet were he, as you paint him, thus complete,
And fond to lay his garlands at your feet,
Sure young men's minds ftill fubject are to
    change,
Though from our plains he were not doom'd
    to range.
A change of fcenes may, with diftorted brows,
Pour fwift contempt on all your former vows.
But let indiff'rence lodge within your breaft,
Nor Strephon's abfence e'er your mind mo-
    left;
The more his charms, the furer he'll fucceed
'Mong pow'rful rivals, whom you now may
    dread.

ALMEDA.

I know his charms the gentleft dame might
    move,
But he'll admit no rival in his love:
My image ftill remains within his breaft,
True to that hour I firft my love confeft.
This pleafing hope will foothe my anxious
    foul,
Nor let ftern care its peaceful fway controul,

Diffufe into my heart its foft relief,

Difpel my fears and diffipate my grief.

I'll fay the youth, for me by heaven defign'd,

Is good, as lovely, conftant, as he's kind ;

So fmoothly fhall the feafons glide along,

Till Strephon's prefence animate my fong,

Then fhall my pleafure as my love abound,

'Till Hymen's rites with pureft joys be
    crown'd.

FLAVIA.

So may you fing, and figh your years away,

With flatt'ring hope, perch'd on the feeble
    fpray

Of Strephon's faith, the efforts rend'ring vain

Of fuch as would effay your love to gain,

Till his own choice, or fome difafter fhow,

Your promis'd pleafures vanifh'd like the
    fnow.

Your charms are fled, no lover then in view,

The paths of difcontent you will purfue.

That you defpis'd Philander then you'll
    mourn,

Nor gave Lothario's fuit a juft return;

Or for Alonzo figh when 'tis too late,
And with reluctance meet your deftin'd fate.
This will your flighted lovers laugh to fee
Almeda then a maiden old will be.

ALMEDA.

The paths you paint I will not tread alone,
While Flavia lives I fhall be fure of one.
Then hand in hand we'll fmooth the rugged
      way,
And figh for figh fhall bear our griefs away.

FLAVIA.

Why fhould we figh? In fmiles we will con-
      tend,
And laugh at what we have no power to
      mend.
Should fate deprive me of my darling fwain,
Some braver youth perhaps may grace the
      plain,
And make me happy by the nuptial band,
When cheerfully he gives his heart and hand.
Or if defpis'd and unadmir'd I reft,
I'll call my own fad deftiny the beft.

I'll blifs the fate I oft have fought to fhun,
And fcorn the fool who would to wedlock
    run.
See Nature now in contraft with thy grief;
The warbling fongfters feem to chant relief;
Their notes are cheerful, nor with fighs de-
    prefs'd;
In concert join and foothe your cares to reft.

ALMEDA.

Nor warblers can give me delight,
   How mournful and penfive their ftrain;
Nought fweet can appear to my fight,
   Since Strephon's forfaken the plain.

With joy I thefe banks did furvey,
   With pleafure I've por'd on the ftream:
Young Strephon then with me did ftray,
   And of nought but delight I could dream.

While he by my fide did recline,
   The flowers feem'd to brighten their bloom;
The fun with more luftre did fhine,
   And fragrance the fields did perfume.

Still pleas'd with his whifpers of love,
　　Still charm'd with his amorous tale;
Now beauty's forfaken the grove,
　　And his abfence I'll ever bewail.

How gloomy and difmal the fhade,
　　Where Strephon was wont to appear,
Where oft his addreffes he made,   ·
　　And his accents delighted my ear.

Thofe paths I revifit in pain;
　　Yet love them without knowing why.
When fortune no favour will deign,
　　I deem it a pleafure to figh.

In vain have my vifitants ftrove
　　My woes to divert by a fmile;
Though I feem'd of their jeft to approve,
　　My heart was with Strephon the while.

Society, fpoil'd of each charm,
　　Without him no pleafure can give;
In folitude cares will alarm,
　　In his abfence 'tis painful to live.

When Sol, from the watery main,
  Afcends to illumine the fky,
My thoughts to the lovelieft fwain,
  More fwift than the lightning can fly.

I mufe on his charms all the day;
  The theme feems enchantingly fweet,
Nor ends with bright Phœbus's ray;
  In dreams I my wifhes repeat.

Ye angels that fuccour the brave,
  Prove guardians to the fweet youth;
Still may he with honour behave,
  Integrity, wifdom and truth.

While through diftant climes he may rove,
  His image is fix'd in my view;
Let Strephon be conftant in love,
  And Almeda will ever be true.

THE SPRING.

NOW winter, reluctant, the fway
   Refigns to the genial fpring;
Sol fheds an enlivening ray,
   And warblers delightfully fing.

Frefh verdure adorns the gay plains,
   So lately o'er-mantl'd with fnow;
The rivers, releas'd from their chains,
   Do now with foft murmuring flow.

The lark and the linnet unite,
   The Cuckow too joins in the lay;
All nature's profufe of delight,
   And foft fanning zephyrs now play.

How charming the garden appears?
  Sweet primrofes paint the gay vale:
Its head now the daffodil rears,
  The fweeteft of feafons to hail,

His team now the hind drives along;
  Quite cheerful he ploughs the rude plain.
He hums his love's praife in a fong,
  Or whiftling forgets her difdain.

The feed in the furrow he throws,
  Indulg'd by bright Phœbus's rays;
Rich Ceres vaft increafe beftows,
  When Autumn her bounty difplays.

The lambkins now fport on the mead;
  They fkip round the heath-cover'd hill;
Their dams how fecurely they feed
  By the fide of yon murm'ring rill?

Near Damon appears with his lute,
  And wakes the melodious lay;
The fongfters, attentive and mute,
  Are perch'd on the wav'ring fpray.

F

As Phillis traverfes the grove,
    All nature more charming appears:
Leander's foft ftories of love,
    Still touchingly found in her ears.

They hand in hand trip o'er the plain;
    No couple more cheerful and gay:
She counts him the lovelieft fwain;
    He calls her the Queen of the May.

Of each others hearts they are fure;
    The arts of no rival they dread.
From minds fo unfulli'd and pure,
    No treachery e'er can proceed.

Few princes partake of fuch joys,
    Remov'd from all faction and ftrife:
Sure riches and honours are toys,
    But their's the endearments of life.

YOUNG William once the blitheſt of
      the ſwains,
That grac'd the flow'ry bank, or trode the
      plains;
Not ruſtic, but from affectation free,
Still courteous, kind, and affable was he.
Of gentleſt manners, ever form'd to pleaſe;
His mind unruffl'd, ever bleſt with eaſe;
His mien engaging, ſweet beyond compare;
His breath delicious as the fragrant air;
His nature prone, attractive ſweets t' impart,
Good without ſhew, and lovely without art.

   Each nymph him priz'd, and oft they
      fought, in vain,
The noble conqueſt of his heart to gain,

Their gentleſt arts unable were to move,
His ſoul ſerene, yet undiſturb'd by love.
Ah! tranſient happineſs! how ſhort thy ſway!
How ſwift thy flight! how ſudden thy decay!
Thy abſence now the youth, dejected, mourns,
While in his heart love's kindling paſſion
  burns.

A lovely nymph, adorn'd with ev'ry grace,
Fairer than fam'd, of old, Arcadia's race:
An eaſy ſhape, and graceful in her air,
The virgins' envy, and the ſwains' deſpair.
Her name was Mary, from the banks of Clyde,
She came to taſte the ſummer in its pride.
One fatal eve, this charming youth paſs'd by,
And on this blooming damſel caſt his eye:
Her charms, reſiſtleſs, ſmote his gen'rous
  heart,
Surpris'd, confounded, then he felt the ſmart.
Sometime with wonder on the maid he gaz'd,
Then ſilence broke, and thus, like one amaz'd:
" What do I feel! from whence this magic
  ſpell!
Is this that love of which the poets tell?

It muft be fo; elfe why this pleafing pain,
Thefe fweet enchanting hopes the nymph to
    gain ?
This fear, this dread, which does my foul
    moleft ?
Such things till now were ftrangers to my
    breaft."

He own'd 'twas love, and wifh'd to find
    relief;
But warbling fongfters can't affuage his grief.
The fweets of Spring no pleafure now can
    yield,
Nor all the verdure which adorns the field.
To this foft paffion all his powers gave way,
And in his heart young Mary bore the fway.
Go then, fond youth, and tell the maid thy
    care,
Who knows, perhaps fhe may be kind as fair.
Yes, Mary fure will hear thy plaintive ftrain;
'Twas her who caus'd, fhe too muft cure thy
    pain.
Thy paffion urg'd, *her* tender love confeft,
What maid fo happy, or what fwain fo bleft?

JOIN now Apollo the harmonious ſtrain,
   O Muſes, Graces, all ye gentle train;
Once more conſpire to aid my humble lays,
And wake my harp to fam'd Lothario's praiſe.
A comely youth, young Cupid's favourite
     care,
Handſome in ſhape, and graceful in his air:
In all reſpects he's form'd the fair to pleaſe,
Can ſigh, and talk, and laugh, and love with
     eaſe.
But O what words, what numbers can ex-
     preſs,
What muſe can paint Lothario's late diſtreſs?
This I'll eſſay, although the taſk's ſevere,
While Delia drops a ſympathetic tear.

And thus it happen'd, on a fatal morn,
Rous'd with the found of hound and echo-
    ing horn,
This charming youth, on rural fports intent,
With fome companions to the field he went:
Each hound he fummons, they attend him
    there,
With eager fteps purfue the timid hare.
Pleas'd with their toil, o'er various heights
    they went,
Nor did the craggy cliffs their fpeed prevent.
Too foon Lothario gain'd the wifh'd for prize,
While horns and hounds re-echo to the fkies.

The chafe now paft, their late infpiring
    toil,
Our jovial fportfman led to reft a while.
To the next inn with hafty fteps they pafs,
And quaff with focial hearts the cheerful glafs.
In foaming goblets pleafing draughts went
    round;
In fparkling liquors ev'ry care was drown'd.
But ah! the fumes affect Lothario's brain;
Once more he tries for pleafure on the plain.

The ſcene is chang'd, his pleaſure now is
  gone,
Loſt and forlorn he wanders all alone.
With weari'd ſteps, o'er barren heaths he paſt,
And in Bane's moſs, alas! he lands at laſt.
His trembling hand, which held the lifeleſs
  hare,
Now caſts it from him as not worth his care.
Three times he drops, three times he lifts his
  plaid,
Hope and deſpair by turns his breaſt invade:
He look'd for help, alas! no help was nigh,
And in the dreary moſs he's forc'd to lie.
" Am I to Death become an eaſy prey,"
With quiv'ring lips methought he thus did
  ſay,
" Now farewell hope, my much lov'd friends,
  adieu;
" My dear companions, charming Delia too.
" O wert thou near to heave a tender ſigh,
" Upon thy breaſt I would contented die:
" With raviſh'd eyes I'll view thy charms
  no more;
" My race is run, life's fleeting viſion o'er."

Thus did the sad Lothario vent his grief,
Till balmy sleep bestow'd a short relief.
On mossy pillows rests his drooping head,
While azure curtains hang around his bed.
All night expanded on the turf he lay,
Nor op'd his eyes till dawning of the day:
The chilling frost his tender form had seiz'd,
But Phœbus' beams the captive swain releas'd,
Abash'd, confounded, being thus confin'd,
To free himself part of his coat resign'd;
With tardy pace the plains he wander'd o'er,
Some cot or village wish'd to see once more.
Kind fortune now did her assistance lend,
And led him safely to a gen'rous friend.

Lothario view'd the mansion with delight,
And at the door he knock'd with all his might.
Impatience, by repeated strokes, confest,
Till they with joy receiv'd the welcome guest,
Who seem'd as one from mortals long
          estrang'd,
His soft address and comely visage chang'd:
His clothes by nauseous mud bespatter'd o'er;
His hair dishevell'd, and his ruffles tore.

Struck with amaze, they view'd his difmal
  cafe,
Nor were they flow in rend'ring him folace.
Unto the parlour fire he firft is led,
From thence into Matilda's downy bed;
Then with affiduous care they kindly foothe
And cheer the lonely, wand'ring, helplefs
  youth.
Each friendly aid confpir'd to eafe his pain,
And bring Lothario to himfelf again.

Ye lovely nymphs, now fing in fofteft
  ftrains
Lothario's praife, the pride of Scotia's plains;
Ye charming youths, bleft with his company,
Pray that Bane Mofs he never more may fee.

A M A N D A:

AN ELEGY

ON THE

DEATH OF Mrs. ——,

PERSONATING HER HUSBAND.

Where can the wretched find relief
    from wo,
Or fue for comfort in life's dreary vale?
Here can philofophy no aid beftow,
And reafon muft in all her efforts fail.

What bofom feels not, while with deepeft
    fighs,
In fault'ring accents, I of Fate complain?
A pale and mangl'd corps Amanda lies;
O that by favage hands fhe had been flain!

It was her own, on fatal purpofe bent,
To dark oblivion be the deed confign'd;
Nor let officious mem'ry thus torment,
With wild reflection my diforder'd mind.

Ah! what is happinefs? an airy dream:
While ftupid mortals fondly hope its ftay,
Supinely bafking in the tranfient gleam,
A fudden blaft difpels the glimm'ring ray.

Amanda, late the faireft of the throng,
Of all our rural nymphs fhe was the pride:
I faw, I lov'd, nor did I languifh long,
With modeft blufhes fhe became my bride.

We then the fweets of focial life did prove,
Bleft in our lot, nor did we figh for fame.
A comely boy, the pledge of mutual love,
Enhanc'd our pleafure, and our care did claim.

What words can paint the horrors of my
          breaft,
While briefly I the tragic fcene difclofe?
Pale death our darling infant did arreft,
One direful night when funk in foft repofe.

No tender guardian mark'd his lateſt ſigh;
No cordial did his quiv'ring lips receive;
So have I ſeen a flow'r of faireſt die,
Bud in the morn, and fade before 'twas eve.

Amanda view'd the change with wild ſur-
   priſe;
Tumult'ous paſſions did her boſom ſwell;
Nor could ſhe long the fervid flame diſguiſe;
An awful victim to deſpair ſhe fell!

She's gone, and Nature ſeems a blank to me;
No charm appears in all its large domain.
The ſongſters ſilent ſit upon the tree,
Or pour their notes in melancholy ſtrain.

The banks of Irvine yield me no delight,
Nor can bright Phœbus cheer me by his ray:
In reſtleſs toſſing ſtill I ſpend the night,
Nor comfort find at the return of day.

The briny tears in copious torrents flow,
Nor can my trembling hand the theme purſue:
The pangs I feel may Damon never know;
Amanda's gone, my deareſt friend adieu.

CELIA

AND

HER LOOKING GLASS.

———

AS Celia, who a coquette was,
 O'er fading charms lamented,
She frown'd upon her looking-glafs,
 And thus her fpleen fhe vented.

" Thou filly, ftupid, worthlefs thing,
 Of all difcretion empty,
I o'er the window will thee fling,
 If any more you tempt me.

Thou'rt incorrigible and bold,
 Unworthy my attention :
What! muft I ever more be told,
 The thing I dread to mention?

A maiden old, kind heaven avert;
   I hate the appellation.
The blood runs chill about my heart,
   I'm choak'd with fore vexation.

Laſt night when at the ball I danc'd,
   My air was counted charming;
My eyes gave pain where'er they glanc'd,
   Each geſture prov'd alarming.

Philander ſaw, their pow'r confeſt,
   And with love tales did teaſe me!
I ſigh'd, I frown'd, he was diſtreſs'd,
   But with my ſmiles ſeem'd eaſy.

But Chloe mark'd, that new made toaſt,
   By other flirts ſurrounded,
Poor Celia now her charms had loſt,
   Which in laſt cent'ry wounded.

A whiſper then and laugh went round,
   Such ſcoffing I endured,
Nor did Philander heed my frown,
   But by the jeſt was cured.

An eafy paffage through the crowd
    I found, none did efcort me;
No gallant youth my prefence fu'd,
    Nor flatter'd to fupport me.

Now Morpheus next I did addrefs,
    For flumbers more delightful;
But in my dreams I found diftrefs,
    With apes and fpectres frightful.

Then unto thee, thou bafe ingrate,
    I fu'd for confolation,
Who rudely now foretels my fate
    Without alleviation.

Though I'm abandon'd on that fcore,
    Though fools and fops are changed,
Of thy impertinence no more,
    Elfe fure I'll be revenged."

Its head the looking-glafs did bow,
    With reverent low fubmiffion,
And to its angry miftrefs now,
    Did utter this petition.

" O ma lam, deign to hear my tale,
   And let my forrows move ye;
My plain fincerity can't fail
   To fhew how much I love you.

Nor lap-dog, bird, or powder'd beau
   Was more by you regarded,
Than I full fifteen years ago,
   Though bafely now difcarded.

Each hour you paid me, vifits ten,
   My counfel well you trufted;
Without my approbation then
   No curls you e'er adjufted.

An artlefs fmile adorn'd your cheek,
   And grac'd each lovely feature,
Which I obferve now, once a-week,
   Diftorted by ill nature.

The pallid cheek and wrinkl'd brow
   Announce your charms declining;
And wont you take the veftal vow
   Without fo much repining?

G

The truth, though in unwelcome ſtrain,
　　To you I muſt diſcover;
While youth or beauty ſways the ſwain,
　　You'll never find a lover."

Poor Celia now could bear no more,
　　Her ſtars malignant curſed;
Her looking-glaſs caſt on the floor,
　　And into tears ſhe burſted.

She would have died, but Claudia came,
　　Preventing all her fears;
He wed the penſive, weeping dame,
　　And wip'd away her tears.

UNFORTUNATE RAMBLER.

———◆———

LATE on an evening I chanced to roam,
 The night it was dark, and the ſtreets
  they were dirty;
It was to attend the lov'd Celia home,
 Engag'd in a company jovial and hearty.

I inſtantly haſten'd to put on my ſhield,
 The ſhield of indiff'rence, perhaps you
  may know it;
Appriz'd of the danger attending the field,
 I judg'd it a piece of high prudence to
  ſhew it.

I went to the door of an elegant inn ;
    I heard who was there, and was fearful to
        venture :
Hope to embolden me then did begin,
    And courage undaunted advis'd me to en-
        ter.

I quickly stepp'd forward, but struck with
    amaze,
    By imminent danger I then was surround-
        ed:
Three handsome young damsels upon me
    did gaze,
    And all of a sudden, alas! I was wounded.

Their shafts were set right, and their arrows
    did fly ;
    I scarce could distinguish from whom they
        came thickest.
By Cupid's assistance at last I did spy
    The person best tim'd in her motions, and
        quickest.

Each gefture was killing, and gave me furprife;
 I grop'd for my breaft-plate, it from me
  was taken:
My fhield of indiff'rence had left me like-
  wife;
 My courage did fail, and my heart it was
  fhaken.

Thus finding myfelf in a pitiful plight;
 A young maid fo handfome I needs muft
  admire:
I gave a deep figh, and I bid them goodnight;
 My only expedient was—to retire.

A little of abfence effected the cure,
 So happily I of my wounds did recover;
But now at a diftance to keep I'll be fure,
 And laugh at the fate of a vanquifhed
  lover.

L U C I N A.

AN ELEGY.

DIREFUL indeed are thy effects, O love!
 When Reafon's voice deferts thy fran-
  tic fhrine;
Platonic leffons no afylum prove;
His dictates muft obfequious yield to thine.

Religion, in majeftic form array'd,
Attempts to foothe the wild, diforder'd breaft.
Alas! too often fails the promis'd aid,
Nor can procure one tranquil moment's reft.

The wife, fubdu'd by thy tyrannic fway,
Thy cruel and malignant influence feel;
Compell'd to act by thy delufive ray,
As humble vot'ries at thine altars kneel.

The Prince, the Peasant, drag an equal chain,
Nor high, nor low, thy subtle darts can brave.
Lucina felt the agonizing pain,
Then hopeless sunk amid the rapid wave.

She was of Annon's lovely nymphs the grace,
Of charms superior to the crowd possess'd :
Her shape was faultless, matchless fair her
        face,
Her virtues bright, by Envy's self confest.

Of all the sprightly youths that sought to gain
The envi'd conquest of her virgin heart,
Philander prov'd the dear distinguish'd swain,
Arm'd with the cruel, unrelenting dart.

He in soft accents urg'd his ardent flame,
And when Lucina would his suit deny,
Her beating bosom would assert his claim—
Her modest blush, and more expressive eye.

At last her tongue, the purpose of her heart
Unto the youth convey'd, in tender strain :
Then mutual joy each whisper did impart,
So great the transport, neither dream'd of pain.

But Ah! their joys were foon for ever loft,
Her fire, enrag'd, forbid the nuptial tie,
Becaufe Philander no rich ftores could boaft;
Charms moft attractive to a parent's eye.

The injur'd youth was by refentment fway'd;
To this his fofter paffion foon gave way:
Too rafh, alas! he fought another maid,
And left Lucina to defpair a prey.

From ev'ry hope, from all her wifhes torn,
Depriv'd of what alone could give relief,
The lovely fair, dejected and forlorn,
Some time in heavy fighs did vent her grief,

The nymphs affembling us'd their utmoft art,
The fad Lucina's forrows to beguile:
Vain was th' attempt to eafe her bleeding
          heart,
Or from her eye extort a cheerful fmile.

At lateft hour, when each aufpicious light
Seem'd hid in chaos—Cynthia's filver beam
Withdrew its luftre on that fatal night,
Nor blefs'd the fhade, nor wanton'd in the
      ftream.

Her auburne locks the mournful maiden
    tore,
Her downy pillow could afford no reft;
She wander'd where the fwelling furges roar,
In wild defpair fhe beat her fnowy breaft!

From Annon's cliff, fhe view'd the breaking
    wave;
Philander was her laft, her darling theme;
No hand was near the frantic maid to fave,
And, Sappho-like, love's victim fhe became!

Ye rigid parents, with attentive ear,
Inftruction learn from this fad tale of wo:
Ye heedlefs maids, in time the danger fear,
That wrought Lucina's fatal overthrow.

ENVIED KISS.

AND was it thine to ſhare the blifs,
  For which ſo many ſigh in vain?
And did thy lips receive a kiſs
  From James that honeſt-hearted ſwain?

Oft has Belinda tri'd her art,
  In this her radiant charms did fail;
Oft Sylvia ſought to touch his heart,
  But could not in the leaſt prevail.

Oft Chloe ſung in tender ſtrain,
  Califta danc'd upon the green;
But James in haſte tripp'd o'er the plain,
  And ſeem'd as though he had not ſeen.

Ulysses-like, he did defy
 The Syren's moft enchanting voice;
In vain Matilda's fparkling eye
 Did labour hard to fix his choice.

Thou little, happy, fmiling fair,
 And didft thou then the victor prove?
Is James now caught in Cupid's fnare,
 And taught by thee to kifs and love?

If in thy early infant ftate,
 Thou mak'ft fuch ftubborn hearts to yield,
What conquefts do thy charms await,
 When ripen'd beauties grace the field?

Does baleful Envy rear its creft,
 For this one favour now obtain'd?
Sure rage will fwell each female breaft,
 When o'er mankind thy empire's gain'd.

Then gentle charmer pity have,
 Nor figh for conquefts ever new:
In hafte fome fond Amyntor fave,
 And let us hear no more of you.

YOUNG MAN'S RESOLUTION.

BY Cupid and Bacchus I'm fadly perplex'd,
　　Both parties to hear I incline:
The urchin for ever comments on this text,
　　Beware of the juice of the vine.

Then Bacchus appears, with a cup in his hand,
　　Says, " Drink, and you'll drown ev'ry care;
But mind, ere you tafte, I'll a promife demand,
　　That you fly from the lips of the fair."

O, fad the dilemma! pray, what muft I do?
　　With Bacchus I never can part:
Ah! dear little God, if neglected by you,
　　It will rend ev'ry ftring of my heart.

O why fuch a pother? I've found out a way,
　　I'll bind myfelf faft by an oath,
While life warms my breaft, each his pow'r
　　　　fhall difplay,
　　And I'll henceforth be loyal to both.

TO A

YOUNG MAN

UNDER SENTENCE OF DEATH

FOR

FORGERY.

FROM HIS MISTRESS.

IN awful folitude, in direful chains,
  Where deep defpair and fad reflection
    reigns,
If yet thy breaft another's woes can feel,
Woes which no language ever can reveal,
Let the diftreffes of a haplefs maid,
Be to thy filent gloomy cell convey'd.
Life left my heart, I felt my blood run cold,
When the fad tidings of thy fate were told:

Then keeneſt anguiſh wrung my tortur'd
    frame,
Diſtraction ſeem'd to ſeize my madd'ning
    brain.
Depriv'd of thee, who could all pain remove,
My heav'n on earth, my happineſs, my love;
Depriv'd of hope, whoſe dear, deluſive ray
Did ſofteſt ſcenes of happineſs, portray:
Scenes now for ever fled! the poignant dart,
Deep wounds my ſoul, and tears my bleed-
    ing heart.

For thee, no more, I'll wait th' appointed
    hour,
No more I'll meet thee in the peaceful bower;
No more, enraptur'd, hang upon thy ſmile,
No more thy preſence ev'ry care beguile.
Was it for me? grant ſupport gracious heav'n!
Was it for me the fatal bond was giv'n?
Is it for me ſtern Juſtice muſt ariſe?
Is it for me he now a victim lies?
Diſtracting thoughts ſtill crowd upon my
    mind!
O were my reſtleſs ſoul to heav'n reſign'd!

O could I now my piercing griefs conceal,
Nor add fresh anguish to the wounds you feel!

'Tis vain, alas! my bursting heart o'erflows,
And death I feel will terminate my woes!
It was for thee alone I wish'd to live;
The world without thee can no pleasure give.
Now law for one rash act thy life demands
Tho' pure till then thy thoughts, unstain'd
   thy hands:
While villains hourly practis'd in deceit,
At freedom range, nor dread impending fate.
Ah! now I fee thee to the fcaffold walk,
I hear the gazing crowd unthinking talk.
Farewell, my love! O still on heaven rely,
I can no more, I tremble, faint and die!

ON

AN UNLOOKED-FOR

SEPARATION FROM A FRIEND.

TRANSIENT proves our fweeteft plea=
 fure,
  Short our moments of delight;
While we grafp the darling treafure,
  O how rapid. is its flight?

Oft at morn ourfelves we flatter,
  That our comforts wont decay;
Fortune lavifh feems to fcatter
  Faireft flowers along.our way.

But the change by night is galling;
  We lament our doom fevere:
Joys, like fnows on Ailfa falling,
  In a moment difappear.

Such the plague of human nature,
  · Fond to trifle with our smart,
While we do escape the greater,
  Little evils rend our heart.

I have lost no valu'd charter,
  Nor lament a fickle swain;
But, alas! a friend's departure,
  Fills my heart with piercing pain.

Pond'ring sharpens ev'ry arrow,
  Sighing but augments my grief:
Now I mourn, o'erwhelm'd with sorrow,
  But next hour may bring relief.

H

JANUARY FIRST, 1792.

TO-DAY old wrinkl'd Time appears;
   A ſmile adorns his brow,
While to our liſt of fleeting years,
   He adds the ninety-two.

Our fav'rite hopes, that ſwiftly glide,
   Announce his ſteps too ſlow,
Leſt Diſappointment's haſty ſtride
   Should ev'ry blifs o'erthrow.

He ſoftly creeps along the way,
   While we his progreſs watch:
He turns his back, vain our eſſay
   His bald-pate then to catch.

On his right hand a lovely dame,
   In robes of crimfon hue;
Her eyes our admiration claim,
   Her form attracts our view;

Diftant her air, ftaid, fapient, mild,
   A figure fine and tall;
By Wifdom own'd, her legal chi'd,
   Who did her Prudence call.

With vermil lips, in accents fweet,
   Soft as that falling fnow,
Thefe words I heard the nymph repeat,
   Addrefs'd to all below:

" In Virtue's caufe exert your pow'rs,
   Let her your actions fway;
Employ with fpeed the paffing hours,
   Nor truft another day."

On his left hand, with tardy pace,
   Here walks a maid forlorn;
Lank hunger painted on her face,
   Her fcanty raiment torn:

H 2

Rich Luxury her father deem'd,
 Idle her dam confefs'd;
In public by no man efteem'd,
 In fecret much carefs'd.

With fmirking fmile, and fpeeches fair,
 She does us kindly greet;
But fage Experience cries, " Beware!
 She'll prove an arrant cheat."

This now the lazy warrior finds,
 His fword with ruft adorn'd;
Half plann'd as yet his dire defigns,
 His conquefts unperform'd.

She'll fpoil the politician's fcheme,
 The patriot's gen'rous toil;
For Sloth is the impoftor's name,
 O deign her not a fmile.

She whifper'd in young Strephon's ear,
 When Delia feem'd to frown,
That foon fhe'd change that lock fevere,
 And all his wifhes crown.

Lull'd in her foft, alluring chain,
    His fuccefs did prevent;
Till Delia found an active fwain,
    And left him to lament.

Poor Chloe's comrade, air and late,
    While pow'rs fhe had to charm;
Thofe gone, fhe feels the fad deceit,
    And gives the loud alarm.

In vain each fpecious art fhe tries;
    Vain the cofmetic aid:
She muft be what all ranks defpife,
    An old forfaken maid.

Sloth, of fociety the peft,
    Of ev'ry blifs the bane,
May we the latent ills deteft,
    Which form thy direful train.

Our helm let Prudence ever fteer;
    She'll fhield us from the blaft;
And ev'ry new, revolving year,
    Remind us of our laft.

H 3

Direct our courſe to yonder ſhore,
　　Where virtue ever reigns;
Where time and ſeaſons are no more;
　　Where death is bound in chains.

Unvari'd there the bliſsful ſcene,
　　'Mid ſeraphims above,
All pure, all placid, and ſerene,
　　All harmony and love.

ON A

VISIT TO Mr. BURNS.

IS't true? or does some magic spell
   My wond'ring eyes beguile?
Is this the place where deigns to dwell
   The honour of our isle?

The charming BURNS, the Muse's care,
   Of all her sons the pride;
This pleasure oft I've sought to share,
   But been as oft deni'd.

Oft have my thoughts, at midnight hour,
   To him excursions made;
This bliss in dreams was premature,
   And with my slumbers fled.

H 4

'Tis real now, no vifion here
    Bequeaths a poignant dart ;
I'll view the poet ever dear,
    Whofe lays have charm'd my heart.

Hark! now he comes, a dire alarm
    Re-echoes through his hall!
Pegafus * kneel'd, his rider's arm
    Was broken by a fall.

The doleful tidings to my ears
    Were in harfh notes convey'd ;
His lovely wife flood drown'd in tears,
    While thus I pond'ring faid :

" No cheering draught, with ills unmix'd,
    Can mortals tafte below ;
All human fate by heav'n is fix'd,
    Alternate joy and wo."

With beating breaft I view'd the bard ;
    All trembling did him greet :
With fighs bewail'd his fate fo hard,
    Whofe notes were ever fweet.

       * The name of the Poet's horfe.

GIVEN TO A LADY

WHO ASKED ME TO WRITE

A POEM.

IN royal Anna's golden days,
    Hard was the taſk to gain the bays:
Hard was it then the hill to climb;
Some broke a neck, ſome loſt a limb.
The vot'ries for poetic fame,
Got aff decrepit, blind, an' lame:
Except that little fellow Pope,
Few ever then got near its top:
An' Homer's crutches he may thank,
Or down the brae he'd got a clank.

    Swift, Thomſon, Addiſon, an' Young
Made Pindus echo to their tongue,

In hopes to pleafe a learned age;
But Doctor Johnfton, in a rage,
Unto pofterity did fhew
Their blunders great, their beauties few.
But now he's dead, we weel may ken;
For ilka dunce maun hae a pen,
To write in hamely, uncouth rhymes;
An' yet forfooth they pleafe the times.

A ploughman chiel, Rab Burns his name,
Pretends to write; an' thinks nae fhame
To foufe his fonnets on the court;
An' what is ftrange, they praife him for't.
Even folks, wha're of the higheft ftation,
Ca' him the glory of our nation.

But what is more furprifing ftill,
A milkmaid muft tak up her quill;
An' fhe will write, fhame fa' the rabble!
That think to pleafe wi' ilka bawble.
They may thank heav'n, auld Sam's afleep:
For could he ance but get a peep,
He, wi' a vengeance wad them fen'
A' headlong to the dunces' den.

Yet Burns, I'm tauld, can write wi' eafe,
An' a' denominations pleafe;
Can wi' uncommon glee impart
A ufefu' leffon to the heart;
Can ilka latent thought expofe,
An' Nature trace whare'er fhe goes:
Of politics can talk wi' fkill,
Nor dare the critics blame his quill.

But then a ruftic country quean
To write—was e'er the like o't feen?
A milk maid poem-books to print;
Mair fit fhe wad her dairy tent;
Or labour at her fpinning wheel,
An' do her wark baith fwift an' weel.
Frae that fhe may fome profit fhare,
But winna frae her rhyming ware.
Does fhe, poor filly thing, pretend
The manners of our age to mend?
Mad as we are, we're wife enough
Still to defpife fic paultry ftuff.

" May fhe wha writes, of wit get mair,
An' a' that read an ample fhare
Of candour ev'ry fault to fcreen,
That in her dogg'ral fcrawls are feen."

All this and more, a critic faid;
I heard and flunk behind the fhade:
So much I dread their cruel fpite,
My hand ftill trembles when I write.

EPISTLE.

TO NELL,

WROTE FROM

LOUDOUN CASTLE.

———————————

DEAR Nell with your long filence griev'd,
 Your welcome miffive I receiv'd,
And have in hafte tane up the pen,
Some incoherent rhyme ro fen':
As time for ftudy is but fcarce,
Accept extemporary verfe.

 To Loudoun Caftle well I got;
It is a moft delightfu' fpot.
The houfe, tho' built before the flood,
Remains as yet both firm and good:

The more to decorate the place,
Our parents do the portals grace.
There Adam ſtands, a comely man,
Eve wi' the apple in her han':
In Eden's yard the fruit was ſweet,
But here ſhe has not got it eat.

A garden large, and hedges high,
O'er which an eagle ſcarce could fly;
Odorif'rous flowers of vari'd hue,
In ilka bord'ring walk we view.
Trees in full bloom, whoſe fruits excel,
When ripe, the roſe's fragrant ſmell;
The plains a pleaſing proſpect yield,
And plenty decks the fertile field.
Each beauteous arbour forms a ſhade,
As if for contemplation made.
The trees in ſtately rows appear,
And ev'ry thing ſeems charming here;
Did not the hungry raven's throat
So far outvie the blackbird's note;
Did not the ill forboding owl,
At midnight, from dark caverns howl.

But Nell, in human life you know,
Our fweets are ever mix'd with wo.
In vain for happinefs we fue,
While as the meteor keeps in view,
With hearts elate, we grafp the prize;
The charm is fled, the phantom dies!
What ftock foe'er the mifers have,
The heart will ever fomething crave;
Which, when poffeft, not foothes the mind,
But leaves an anxious blank behind.
What tho' no bags of gold we've got?
We may be happy in our lot;
And with our little ftill content,
Our all perhaps will ne'er be fpent:
And while we fomething have in ftore,
Why fhould we figh or pine for more?

NELL'S ANSWER.

WHILE you, my friend, in beauteous,
      rural lay,
The ancient pile, and circling scenes display,
Enthusiastic rapture fires my soul,
And admiration reigns without controul.
Methinks, while I your charming theme pur‑
      sue,
That Loudoun castle rises to my view.
I see, or is it fancy that portrays?
The prospect stand before my ardent gaze:
Surpris'd I see a new Elysium rise,
In pomp august, before my wond'ring eyes.

    With joy I view the sweetly, vari'd scene,
The winding vale, and groves of vernal green.
The garden will my fancy long detain,
And those fair fields that wave with yellow
      grain.

The blooming trees that form a sylvan shade,

And those sweet bow'rs for contemplation
made.

Would some propitious pow'r but grant my
boon,

Send some kind genii with an air-balloon;

Take me aloft, and safe convey with care,

Straight to the bonny blooming banks of Air,

To Loudoun castle soon I'd bend my way,

And all its beauties joyfully survey.

The gothic structure, and its fair domains,

Most amply would compensate all my pains.

With you, dear Jenny, I would pass some
hours,

Amongst its shady walks and fragrant bow'rs.

Of poetry and poets talk by turns,

And pleas'd make comments on the far-
fam'd Burns.

EPISTLE TO NELL.

<hr />

WHILE Phœbus did our ſummer ar-
    bours cheer,
And joys Autumnal crown'd our circling
    year;
Even then my thoughts to you excurſions
    made,
And ardently the bypaſt ſcenes ſurvey'd;
Where oft we met in Eccles' peaceful bow'rs,
While ſocial pleaſure mark'd the paſſing hours.
From theſe ſweet ſcenes I found myſelf re-
    mov'd,
I fear'd no more remember'd or belov'd.

Forgot by Nell, whose friendship seem'd sin-
 cere,
Such cold neglect, who undisturb'd could
 bear?

Mild Autumn now resigns to rougher skies,
And frightful storms, in wild commotion,
 rise.
The tempest howls, while dark December
 reigns,
And scatters desolation o'er the plains.
Just as the sun bursts from the wintry cloud,
Which oft does now his native glory shroud,
Your welcome letter cheers my anxious soul;
For humour, wit, and friendship grace the
 whole.
Well pleas'd I find you on Parnassus' hill;
The more I read, the more I prize your skill.
The Muses coy, you seem to catch with ease,
And unfatigu'd attain the art to please.

Go on, dear Nell, the laureate-wreath pur-
 sue,
In time perhaps you may receive your due.

We'll beat the bushes for the rustic muse,
Where ev'ry dunce her inspiration sues.
'Mongst the vast crowd, let you and I aspire
To share a little of Apollo's fire.
If Fortune prove, like Cupid, ever blind,
We may perhaps some petty favour find ;
But if no more we gain by these our lays,
We'll please ourselves with one another's
            praise.

AN EPISTLE

TO A LADY.

November, 1789.

WHILE Morcham does your much
       lov'd prefence fhare,
And Lydia's health claims your maternal care,
O Madam, deign with candour to perufe
A ruftic lay, prefented by the Mufe.
From Loudoun's plains fhe now awakes the
       lyre,
And gladly would to arduous feats afpire.
On the fmooth margin of the ftream reclin'd,
She fondly hopes to pleafe a tafte refin'd.
What tho' fhe boaft of no peculiar charm,
That would the critic of his force difarm?
She humbly deprecates your doom fevere,
And fain would wifh to find you partial here.

The Mufe alone does this indulgence claim,
Elfe it were impious fuch a thought to frame.

Would you from Morcham caft your men-
    tal eye,
And the recefles of our caftle fpy,
You'd fee Honoria, in her elbow chair,
A mind at eafe, thoughts unperplex'd with
    care ;
With afpect mild, explore the facred page,
Guide of her youth, and comfort of her age:
In conduct prudent, and in counfel wife ;
Her friendfhip ev'ry virtuous mind muft
    prize.
Then view the pair, in bonds of Hymen bleft,
With little Cupid's flutt'ring round their
    breaft.
The blifs that's mutual, all their thoughts
    employ,
Whofe focial hearts partake no felfifh joy.
To pleafe each other proves their conftant
    aim,
While ev'ry act endears the tender claim.

Matilda too, your notice muſt demand ;
To paint would here require a Raphael's
     hand :
To trace the radient beauties of her mind,
Shall be a taſk for nobler pens aſſign'd.
I'd rather far her little foibles ſcan,
Though ſtrict inſpection finds no more than
     one.
Such anxious care on others ſhe beſtows,
She quite forgets what to herſelf ſhe owes.
Vouchſafe the charming Celia next a look,
Her mind ſerene, and in her hand a book :
Eyes, which at will, can pleaſure give or pain,
On ſtupid Humphry Clinker ſhine in vain.

As through the hall and kitchen now you
     paſs,
Pray deign to peep among the lower claſs :
The cook's at work ; but, madam, who can
     know
Whether her hands or tongue more ſwiftly go?
They're nimble both ; but diff'rent is th' ef-
     fect ;
One merits praiſe, the other diſreſpect.

Poor Mary fighs beneath a load of woes,
Hard and uneafy ev'ry turn fhe does:
How light foe'er the tafk, fhe'll pond'ring
     fay,
" Ah ! Is there not a lion in the way ?"
Will feems in hafte his mafter's boots to clean,
Old James is driving Turkeys o'er the green,
Our crazy-pated dairy-maid juft now
Is fcribbling o'er thefe fenfelefs lines to you.
Hark ! there's a call, O pardon what I've
     penn'd ;
I'm fure you're glad my letter 's at an end.

FROM

SNIPE,

A FAVOURITE DOG,

TO HIS

MASTER.

————— — —————

May, 1791.

O BEST of good masters, your mild dif-
position
Perhaps may induce you to read my petition:
Believe me in earnest, though acting the poet,
My breast feels the smart, and mine actions
do shew it.

At morn when I rife, I go down to the
    kitchen,
Where oft I've been treated with kicking and
    fwitching.
There's nothing but quiet, no toil nor vexa-
    tion,
The cookmaid herfelf feems poffefs'd of dif-
    cretion.
The fcene gave furprife, and I could not but
    love it,
Then found 'twas becaufe fhe had nothing
    to covet.
From thence to the dining-room I took a
    range fir,
My heart fwells with grief when I think of
    the change there;
No diflres well drefs'd, with their flavour to
    charm me,
Nor even fo much as a fire to warm me.
For bread I ranfack ev'ry corner with caution,
Then trip down the ftair in a terrible paffion.
I go with old James, when the fofs is a dealing,
But brutes are voracious and void of all feel-
    ing;

They quickly devour't; not a morsel they
    leave me,
And then by their growling ill nature they
    grieve me.

My friend Jenny Little pretends to respect
    me,
And yet sir at meal-time she often neglects me:
Of late she her breakfast with me would
    have parted,
But now eats it all, so I'm quite broken
    hearted.
O haste back to Loudoun, my gentle good
    master,
Relieve your poor Snipy from ev'ry disaster.
A sight of yourself would afford me much
    pleasure,
A share of your dinner an excellent treasure,

Present my best wishes unto the good lady,
Whose plate and potatoes to me are ay ready:
When puss and I feasted so kindly together;
But now quite forlorn we condole with each
    other.

No more I'll infift, left your patience be
　　ended;
I beg by my fcrawl, fir, you'll not be offended;
But mind, when you fee me afcending Par-
　　naffus,
The need that's of dogs there to drive down
　　the Affes.

DEATH OF J——. H——. Esq.

JUNE, 1790.

———

ERE Phœbus' beams exhal'd the pearly
    dew,
While hoary moifture all the fields o'erfpread,
Where ozier cyprefs, and the drooping yew,
Had form'd a mufing melancholy fhade.

Belinda fat, bedew'd with briny tears,
The echoing grove her deep-fetch'd fighs re-
    tain;
Her plaintive note diftrefs'd my lift'ning ears,
While in low accents thus fhe did complain.

" And is the pleasing scene, alas! no more!
Corrosive grief now on my vitals prey!
Distrefs'd, in sighs I spend the heavy hour,
Nor feel of comfort one auspicious ray!

Now gloomy visions hover round my bed,
More sadd'ning thoughts my waking hours
   employ!
Hope's balmy whispers are for ever fled,
And far remov'd is ev'ry gleam of joy!

My former days can never more return;
Each future prospect darkens on my view;
Life's rugged paths seem dreary and forlorn;
No kindly hand does there sweet flow'rets
   strew.

Alas! on life's tempestuous ocean toft,
Become a prey to each high swelling wave,
My ev'ry hope of happiness is loft——
Laid in the silent, solitary grave!

No more, O death! thy pointed shafts I dread!
Thy keenest darts I hourly wish to share;
Since my lov'd HENRY's number'd with
   the dead,
Nought in this world can now engage my care!

Ah! what to me avails the radiant fky,
The verdant meadow, or the vocal grove?
No kind companion fhares the melting joy,
And tunes his lute to melody and love.

He was——but oh! no language can ex-
     prefs——
What my lov'd HENRY ever was to me:
My joy in health, my fupport in diftrefs,
My lover, friend, and tender hufband he.

For me a parent's love he did forego,
With all the pleafures of his native fhore:
On me alone did ev'ry care beftow;
He faw me happy, and he wifh'd no more.

Keen recollection animates my pain,
And all my pleafures paft augment my woes;
Yet fond remembrance fhall thofe joys retain,
While vital life within this bofom flows."

Thus fpoke Belinda, on the turf reclin'd;
No ray of hope her fadd'ning fancy cheer'd:
When from a thicket, as by heav'n defign'd,
A nymph celeftial in her fight appear'd.

Her flowing robes wav'd in the ambient air;
A flow'ry wreath her modeft temples grac'd;
Her prefence kindly fmooth'd the brow of
    care,
And all the horrors of the fcene effac'd.

Array'd in heav'nly fmiles fhe onward came;
Vain phantoms her fuperior pow'r confeft:
She view'd the fad, dejected, mournful dame,
And thus in foothing accents her addrefs'd.

" Do not Belinda at thy fate repine,
Nor by thy tears augment the pond'rous load;
The lovely youth muft be no longer thine:
He's gone, fuch is the fov'reign will of God.

He's gone to flourifh in a fairer foil,
A plant too noble for this noxious clime:
Where virtue muft triumphant ever fmile,
He'll fhare of joys extatic and fublime.

Vain are thy forrows, vain the fighs of thofe,
Who did his favour or his friendfhip fhare:
He's gone beyond the reach of human woes,
Above the weight of ev'ry worldly care.

Pure were the virtues center'd in his breaft,
With unaffuming rectitude they fway'd:
His tongue the dictates of his heart exprefs'd,
While his mild manners more than words
    convey'd !

But human blifs is of a tranfient date,
Nor permanent thy woes, tho' now fevere:
Soon fhall you meet in a celeftial ftate,
And then no more the pangs of parting fear,

K

ON THE

BIRTH OF J——. H——. Esq's SON.

NOVEMBER 15, 1790.

DEAR lovely babe, with hearts elate,
   We hail thy natal hour:
Here does the Mufe impatient wait,
   Libations kind to pour.

Upon a theme fo new, fo fweet,
   She now attempts to fing:
No foreign aid fhe needs invite,
   To touch the vocal ftring.

But while with anxious thoughts on thee,
   And ardent look, I gaze,
Can I the valiant hero fee,
   To animate my lays?

The plodding philofophic eye,
   Shall I attempt to fcan?
Or in thy infant fmiles defcry
   The politicians plan?

Too hard the tafk, my humble mufe
   Can boaft of no fuch art;
Though hope, on flutt'ring pinions does
   All this and more impart.

While fondl'd by a mother kind,
   Thou checks the falling tears,
When thy lov'd father to her mind
   In ev'ry charm appears.

The features fweet, attractive, mild,
   Each foft, each winning grace,
She does in thee, her darling child,
   With fond remembrance trace.

And that the virtues he poffefs'd
   May in thy bofom glow,
She does indulgent heav'n requeft,
   Who mitigates her wo.

May he, on whom her hope relies,
   Protect thy lovely form,
While fudden blafts impetuous rife
   In life's tempeftuous ftorm.

For thee, be calm the rolling flood,
   Be ſtill the bluſt'ring wave:
May'ſt thou be bleſs'd with every good
   A mother's heart can crave.

ON A

GENTLEMAN'S

PROPOSING TO TRAVEL 300 MILES

TO SEE J——. H——. Esq:s CHILD.

IS it true! does Alonzo from London pro-
     poſe
   A viſit to Scotia's bleak plain,
Ere the beams of bright Sol have diſperſed
     our ſnows,
   Or the warblers enliven'd their ſtrain?

Does the city prove irkſome, inſipid the ball,
 Nor the theatre claim a delay?
Is it friendſhip or int'reſt that uſhers the call,
 Which he ſeems in ſuch haſte to obey?

I aſk'd, and in whiſpers, by Fame I was told,
 That his heart was by int'reſt unmov'd,
That the ties of pure friendſhip were ſtronger
  than gold,
 And it's exquiſite charms he had prov'd.

But ah! he is gone, whoſe reception ſo kind,
 Would have fully compenſate his toil!
Can the ſight of a babe give ſolace to his mind,
 Or reward the fatigue by a ſmile?

Let the trifling vain clamours of ſtoics be mute,
 While friendſhip directeth the ſcales:
Let them wonder, but never attempt to diſ-
  pute,
 While ſelf o'er their feelings prevails.

In vain let them gueſs what Alonzo muſt
  know,
 Since friendſhip each action inſpires;
His preſence will tend to alleviate wo,
 That done, it is all he deſires.

K 3

WRITTEN ON A FOREIGNER'S VISITING THE GRAVE
OF A SWISS GENTLEMAN, BURIED AMONG THE
DESCENDENTS OF SIR WILLIAM WAL-
LACE, GUARDIAN OF SCOTLAND IN
THE THIRTEENTH CENTURY.

OUR regal feat to Edward fallen a prey,
　　Our Chief's infulted corfe his victim lay;
Our ruin'd land no monument could raife;
Yet grateful bards ftill fung his heart-felt
　　praife.
Long ages hence her hero ftill fhe'll mourn;
Still her brave fons with emulation burn.
His fpirit guarding ftill our native place,
Proclaims this mandate to his lateft race:
" Let facred truth bid living fame be thine;
" Ne'er truft for honour to a fculptur'd
　　fhrine.
" Thofe modeft merits marbles ne'er impart,
" Love writes them deepeft on the human
　　heart."

Thus mid thy race did their lov'd Henry
    dwell,
Whose duft fhall mix thy memory with Tell*:
Truth, honour, fpirit, animate that form,
Which beauty, grace, and fymmetry adorn.
Here that rich bloffom dropp'd, fcarce fairly
    blown;
The friend, the hufband, father we bemoan!
Wail by the grave a mother's cheerlefs throes,
And fhare a widow's agonizing woes!

Dear youth, thy name to lateft time defcends,
Where gentle virtues made mankind thy
    friends.
From no vain marble need you borrow fame;
Truth, love and friendfhip, here embalm
    thy name.
A parent's filver hairs beftrew thy fhrine;
Her griefs were mortal, but her joys fublime:
In tears we mourn the body laid to reft;
She hails thy fpotlefs foul 'mid angels bleft.

* A famous Swifs chief

K 4

PHILANDER TO EUMENES.

WITH pleafure I your welcome letter
   read,
While Cupid for a little from me fled.
With freedom write, difpel your trivial fears;
There's nought prefumptuous in your fong
   appears ;
'Tho' ftrange th' ideas which you now con-
   vey,
While you our lovely females thus portray.

No doubt, there are, in the promifcuous
   crowd,
The worthlefs fair, the virtuous and the good;
The haughty nymph, the maid of humble
   mind ;
'Th' imperious, yea, the gentle and the kind;

Such as an adamantine heart could charm,
And furious tygers of their rage difarm.
In all viciflitudes of human life,
Man's greateft blefling is a virtuous wife:
Her fmiles can't fail to footh his anxious
  breaft,
Diffufing joy, while various cares moleft:
Her prudent counfel fwift relief can bring,
As Abigail appeafed Ifr'el's king.

Nor need I thus the facred annals trace,
In Britain's Ifle they claim the higheft place;
When dire oppreffion, with uplifted hand,
His yoke extended o'er our native land,
Our fires to abject flavery were doom'd, /
Our mothers all their ancient claims refum'd:
You'll fay my fpeeches do me partial prove,
And fo afcribe the cruel caufe to love.
Are you alone exempt from fuch a gueft?
Are you of every antidote poffefs'd
T' effect a cure, or mitigate the pain?
Then may the archer caft his fhafts in vain.

Of late dear friend I did fuch valour boaft;
But by one fatal glance the field was loft.

While you are free of dangers, ftill beware;

Be warn'd by me, and fhun th' alluring
        fnare.

It is by fome deem'd cowardice to fly,

But fure it more ignoble is to die:

To die, I'm frantic, fir; what did I fay?

Reafon once more refume thy wonted fway;

Kind heaven defend us from fuch dire alarms;

Who would a victim fall to female charms?

I find I'm better while your lines I read,

I'm almoft from my Gallic fetters free'd.

As you alone were partner of my grief,

Pray now congratulate my quick relief.

I would not by prolixity offend;

Both bound and free, Philander is your friend.

ARMEDA.

WHY doſt thou Sylvia penſive ſit?
    Why hangs that cloud upon thy brow?
Oft haſt thou cheer'd us by thy wit,
    Why thus reſerv'd and ſullen now?

Haſt thou thy little lap-dog loſt?
    Can Celia's dreſs excite envy?
Is Flavia now the fav'rite toaſt,
    Or doſt thou for a lover ſigh?

SYLVIA.

Be Flavia ſtill the toaſt of beaux;
    Such trifles ne'er could give me pain:
But know the cauſe of all my woes,
    The dear Alonzo's left the plain.

His mufic oft has charm'd the grove;
   So foft his pipe, fo fweet his air:
None heard, but felt the power of love,
   'Mong all the nymphs affembl'd there.

Not Philomel's delightful ftrain
   Could fuch extatic joys impart,
As did thy notes, O darling fwain!
   Which well çan cheer the anxious heart.

His count'nance as Aurora bright,
   His fmiles gave joy to all around:
In virtue, wit, and all that's right,
   Alonzo's equal ne'er was found.

To Anna's banks, alas! he's gone;
   To Eccles fam'd for maidens fair;
And, to augment my grievous moan,
   I dread fome pow'rful rival there.

ARMEDA.

O Sylvia, all your fears are vain;
   I've feen the nymphs difplay their art,
To captivate your charming fwain;
   But none can there engage his heart.

Infensible he seems to grow;
   Defies the little armed boy :
From his lov'd horfe, a fatal throw
   Does more his anxious thoughts employ.

Than Cupid's arrows more fevere,
   The wounds he got his cares now prove :
Can Sylvia think it ftrange to hear
   Alonzo quite forgets to love?

SYLVIA.

Forgets to love! that muft not be;
   Sure Sylvia would be wretched then.
Alonzo, when depriv'd of thee,
   Rough winter ftill deforms the plain.

O haften and difpel my fears!
   The birds with thee more fweetly fing.
O crown with joy revolving years!
   Thy prefence gives perpetual fpring.

CAPTIVATED SOLDIER.

YE fwains unacquainted with love,
 Attend to my pitiful lay :
My pipe fhall refound through the grove,
 And my woes in fad accents difplay.

Long time I with freedom did range ;
 With indiff'rence I gaz'd on the fair :
Now my heart, how affecting the change !
 Matilda has caught in the fnare.

Ah me ! how unlucky the day,
 When thoughtlefs I haften'd to view ?
A wedding was coming this way,
 Nor dream'd I of what did enfue.

Matilda appear'd in her charms;
   Her cheeks with foft blufhes did glow:
My bofom was fill'd with alarms,
   Nor knew I who wounded me fo.

Her fhape it is handfome; her air
   Excels all the nymphs of the town:
Her eyes may with diamonds compare;
   Her locks of the lovelieft brown.

She fwift from my prefence did fly.
   I call'd, but fhe anfwer'd me not:
She fear'd that fome danger might be
   Sly lurking beneath the red coat.

If red will affrighten my dear,
   I'll drefs in the good ruffet grey,
Abandon my fword and my fpear,
   And caft my bright armour away.

No more I'll attend to the drum;
   But take up my fhuttle and weave:
From that fure no danger can come,
   Such clowns have no art to deceive.

No razor fhall come on my face,
   Nor powder be feen on my hair:
I'll walk at no regular pace;
   In brogues to my love I'll repair.

O then, will fhe hear my foft tale?
   O then, will Matilda prove kind?
If ruftics with her can prevail,
   The ruftic in me fhe fhall find.

ON READING

LADY MARY MONTAGUE AND Mrs. ROWE'S

LETTERS.

AS Venus by night, so MONTAGUE bright
    Long in the gay circle did shine:
She tun'd well the lyre, mankind did admire;
    They prais'd, and they call'd her divine.

This pride of the times, in far distant climes,
    Stood high in the temple of Fame:
Britannia's shore, then ceas'd to adore,
    A greater the tribute did claim.

To fue for the prize, fam'd Rowe did arife,
  More bright than Apollo was fhe:
Superior rays obtain'd now the bays,
  And Montague bended the knee.

O excellent Rowe, much Britain does owe
  To what you've ingen'oufly penn'd:
Of virtue and wit, the model you've hit;
  Who reads muft you ever commend.

Would ladies purfue, the paths trod by you,
  And jointly to learning afpire,
The men foon would yield unto them the
    field,   .
  And critics in filence admire.

A YOUNG LADY'S

BREAKING A LOOKING-GLASS.

AS round the room, with tentlefs fpeed,
  Young Delia tripp'd it finely,
A looking-glafs, fo Fate decreed,
  She broke, but not defign'dly.

A looking-glafs of ancient date,
  Its fall the belles lamented ;
But all their forrow prov'd too late,
  Its ruin none prevented.

When Anne the Britifh fceptre fway'd,
  'Twas plac'd in firm pofition ;
Nor did a forward chamber-maid
  E'er alter its condition.

No mirror better could defcry
 Th' embrio of a pimple;
The rheum on a neglected eye;
 The hoary hair or wrinkle.

Long time it did the chimney grace,
 So awkward now and empty;
Its with a vengeance chang'd its place,
 And broke in pieces twenty.

O Delia! mourn thy direful fate,
 A thoufand ills portending!
Black omens now thy ftars await,
 'Gainft which there's no defending.

Poor Delia now, bedew'd with tears
 And piti'd by acquaintance,
Refolv'd to fpend full fifteen years,
 In doleful, deep repentance.

Do tears thefe lovely cheeks diftain,
 By thoufand charms furrounded!
Thefe eyes from weeping do refrain;
 Their glance have many wounded.

'T' adorn thy more accomplish'd mind,
  Each radient grace confpires:
Hence dread thou not their dark defign,
  Though rage each demon fires.

Let hope diffufe a gentle ray,
  Thefe magic fpells defying:
Let prudence Delia's footfteps fway,
  On virtue ftill relying.

But know the rake's alluring fmile,
  The heedlefs fair bewitches:
Let no fond youth your heart beguile,
  By foft enticing fpeeches.

And if good counfel aught avail,
  Attend Diana's claffes:
For mind our fex is ever frail,
  And brittle as our glaffes.

AN

ACROSTIC

UPON A

YOUNG WOMAN,

WRITTEN BY HER LOVER.

HAIL fweeteft charmer of the rural
plain,
Accept the tribute of a humble fwain;
Nor frown, tho' he prefumpt'ous would effay;
No mufe your matchlefs beauties can difplay.
All that is feign'd of the fair Cyprian queen.
Here in this lovely damfel may be feen.
In her fair form is ev'ry grace combin'd;
Virtue and modefty adorn her mind.
If Milton's eloquence did grace my lays,
Sure it would fail, and fpeak but half her
praife.
O Cupid fix an arrow in her breaft!
No more I'd wifh, were I of her poffefs'd.

EXTEMPORARY

ACROSTIC.

MY Mufe, once more, thy aid I humbly
    claim;
Refufe not now to grace my ruftic lays.
Johnfton or Pope might well befit the theme
    Of Grecian bards, who ever merit praife.
How dares my humble hand affume fo high?
    No common character infpires my fong, ,
His growing fame long fince has reach'd the
    fky:
    All I can fay but does his virtues wrong;
Let then my blund'ring pen in filence reft;
Lo, filent admiration paints them beft.

EPISTLE

TO

Mr. *ROBERT BURNS.*

FAIRFA' the honeſt ruſtic ſwain,
   The pride o' a' our Scottiſh plain;
Thou gi'es us joy to hear thy ſtrain,
         And notes ſae ſweet;
Old Ramſay's ſhade, reviv'd again,
         In thee we greet.

Lov'd Thallia, that delightful muſe,
Seem'd long ſhut up as a recluſe:
'To all ſhe did her aid refuſe,
         Since Allan's day,

Till Burns arofe, then did fhe choofe
　　　　To grace his lay.

To hear thy fong, all ranks defire;
Sae well thou ftrik'ft the dormant lyre.
Apollo, wi' poetic fire,
　　　　　Thy breaft did warm,
An' critics filently admire
　　　　　Thy art to charm.

Cæfar an' Luath weel can fpeak;
'Tis pity e'er their gabs fhould fteek:
They into human nature keek,
　　　　　An' knots unravel;
To hear their lectures ance a week,
　　　　　Ten miles I'd travel.

Thy dedication to G—— H——,
In unco bonny, hamefpun fpeech,
Wi' winfome glee the heart can teach
　　　　A better leffon,
Than fervile bards wha fawn an' fleech,
　　　　· Like beggar's meffin.

When flighted love becomes thy theme,
An' woman's faithlefs vows you blame,
With fo much pathos you exclaim,
   In your Lament,
But glanc'd by the moft frigid dame,
   She wad relent.

The daify too, you fing wi' fkill;
An' weel ye praife the whifky gill.
In vain I blunt my fecklefs quill,
   Your fame to raife,
While echo founds, frae ilka hill,
   To Burns's praife.

Did Addifon or Pope but hear,
Or Sam, that critic moft fevere,
A plough-boy fing, wi' throat fae clear,
   They, in a rage,
Their works wad a' in pieces tear
   An' curfe your page.

If I fhould ftrain my rupy throat,
To raife thy praife wi' fwelling note,

My rude, unpolifh'd ftrokes wad blot
    Thy brilliant fhine,
An' ev'ry paffage I would quote
    Seem lefs fublime.

The tafk I'll drop; wi' heart fincere
To heav'n prefent a humble prayer,
That a' the bleflings mortals fhare
    May be, by turns,
Difpens'd with an indulgent care
    To Robert Burns.

MY AUNTY.

MY ever dear an' worthy aunty,
 Wha ne'er o' wit nor lear was vaunty;
Yet often could, like honeſt grandam,
Unravel dreams; an' whiles, at random,
Did truth in myſtic terms declare,
Which made us aft wi' wonder ſtare.

 Laſt night, when Morpheus ſoftly hurl'd
His ſilken ſceptre o'er the world,
Some anxious cares within my breaſt
Were ſilently conſign'd to reſt;
Yet did in ſleep their pow'r retain,
As ſhews the viſions of my brain.

 My works I thought appear'd in print,
And were to diff'rent corners ſent,

Whare patrons kind, but fcant o' fkill,
Had fign'd my fuperfcription bill.
Vorations critics by the way,
Like eagles watching for their prey,
Soon caught the verfe wi' afpeĉt four,
An' did ilk feeble thought devour ;
Nor did its humble, helplefs ftate,
One fraĉtion of their rage abate.

Tom Touchy, one of high pretence
To tafte an' learning, wit an' fenfe,
Was at the board the foremoft man,
Its imperfeĉtions a' to fcan.
Soon as the line he feem'd to doubt,
The meaner critics fcratch'd it out ;
Still to be nam'd on Touchy's fide,
Was baith their int'reft and their pride.

Will Hafty, in an unco rage,
Revis'd the volume page by page ;
But aft was deem'd a ftupid afs,
For cens'ring what alone might pafs.

Jack Tim'rous gladly would have fpoke,
But quiv'ring lips his fentence broke ;

So much he fear'd a brother's fcorn,
The whole efcap'd his claws untorn.

James Eafy calm'd my throbbing heart,
An' whifp'ring told each man apart,
That he the volume much efteem'd;
Its little faults he nothing deem'd:
An' if his vote they would receive,
It might through countlefs ages live.

While I poor James's fpeech admir'd,
Tom Touchy at the found was fir'd:
And ah! it griev'd me much to find,
He prov'd him fenfelefs, deaf, and blind:
Then quick as thought, ere I could tell him,
Ilk critics club was up to fell him;
An' as he, helplefs, met the ftroke,
I, ftarting, trembl'd, fyne awoke.

Now aunty, fee this fad narration,
Which fills my breaft wi' fair vexation;
An' if you can fome comfort gie me,
Make nae delay, but fend it to me:
For I'm commanded by Apollo,
Your fage advice in this to follow.

·*HALLOWEEN.*

SOME folk in courts for pleafure fue,
　　An' fome ranfack the theatre :
The airy nymph is won by few ;
　　She's of fo coy a nature.
She fhuns the great bedaub'd with lace,
　　Intent on rural jokin
An' fpite o' breeding, deigns to grace
　　A merry Airfhire rockin,
　　　　　　　　Sometimes at night.

At Halloween, when fairy fprites
　　Perform their myftic gambols,
When ilka witch her neebour greets,
　　On their nocturnal rambles ;
When elves at midnight-hour are feen,
　　Near hollow caverns fportin,

Then lads an' laffes aft convene,
　　In hopes to ken their fortune,
　　　　　　By freets that night.

At Jennet Reid's not long ago,
　　Was held an annual meeting,
Of laffes fair an' fine alfo,
　　With charms the moft inviting:
Though it was wat, an' wondrous mirk,　·
　　It ftopp'd nae kind intention;
Some fprightly youths, frae Loudoun-kirk,
　　Did hafte to the convention,
　　　　　　Wi' glee that night.

The nuts upon a clean hearthftane
　　Were plac'd by ane anither,
An' fome gat lads, an' fome gat nane,
　　Juft as they bleez'd the gither.
Some fullen cooffs refufe to burn;
　　Bad luck can ne'er be mended;
But or they a' had got a turn,
　　The pokefu' nits was ended
　　　　　　Owre foon that night.

A candle on a 'ftick was hung,
 An' ti'd up to the kipple:
Ilk lad an' lafs, baith auld an' young,
 Did try to catch the apple;
Which aft, in fpite o' a' their care,
 Their furious jaws efcaped;
They touch'd it ay, but did nae mair,
 Though greedily they gaped,
     Fu' wide that night.

The difhes then, by joint advice,
 Were plac'd upon the floor;
Some ftammer'd on the toom ane thrice,
 In that unlucky hour.
Poor Mall maun to the garret go,
 Nae rays o' comfort meeting;
Becaufe fae aft fhe's anfwer'd no,
 She'll fpend her days in greeting,
     An' ilka night.

Poor James fat trembling for his fate;
 He lang had dree'd the worft o't;
Though they had tugg'd and rugg'd till yet,
 To touch the difh he durft not.
     M

The empty bowl, before his eyes,
 Replete with ills appeared;
No man nor maid could make him rife,
 The confequence he feared
     Sae much that night.

Wi' heartfome glee the minutes paft,
 Fach act to mirth confpired:
The cufhion game perform'd at laft,
 Was moft of all admired.
From Janet's bed a boifter came,
 Nor lad nor lafs was miffing;
But ilka ane wha caught the fame,
 Was pleas'd wi' routh o' kiffing,
     Fu' fweet that night.

Soon as they heard the forward clock
 Proclaim 'twas nine, they ftarted,
An' ilka lafs took up her rock;
 Reluctantly they parted,
In hopes to meet fome other time,
 Exempt from falfe afperfion;
Nor will they count it any crime,
 To hae fic like diverfion
     Some future night.

M_{R.} —— *BAKING CAKES.*

———◆———

AS Rab, who ever frugal was,
　　Some oat-meal cakes was baking,
In came a crazy fcribbling lafs,
　　Which fet his heart a-quaking.

" I fear," fays he, " fhe'll verfes write,
　　An' to her neebers fhow it:
But troth I need na care a doit,
　　Though a' the country knew it.

My cakes are good, none can object;
　　The maids will ca' me thrifty;
To fave a fixpence on the peck
　　Is juft an honeft fhifty.

They're fair an' thin, an' crump, 'tis true;
　　You'll own fae when you fee them;
But, what is better than the view,
　　Put out your han' an' pree them."

He fpoke, an' han'd the cakes about,
　　Whilk ev'ry eater prized;
Until the bafket was run out,
　　They did as he advifed.

An' ilka ane that got a fhare,
　　Said that they were fu' dainty;
While Rab cri'd eat, an' dinna fpare;
　　For I hae cakes in plenty.

And i' the corner ftan's a cheefe,
　　A glafs an' bottle by me;
Baith ale and porter, when I pleafe,
　　To treat the laffes flily.

Some ca' me wild an' roving youth;
　　But fure they are miftaken:
The maid wha gets me, of a truth,
　　Her bread will ay be baken.

A

POEM

ON

CONTENTMENT.

INSCRIBED TO JANET NICOL, A POOR OLD WAN-
DERING WOMAN, WHO LIVES BY THE WALL
AT LOUDOUN AND USED SOMETIMES TO
BE VISITED BY THE COUNTESS.

————————

O JANET, by your kind permiffion,
My mufe, in tatter'd low condition,
Would fain attempt, if you'll allow,
To dedicate a fong to you.
Poffefs'd of few attractive pow'rs,
Her cafe does much refemble yours;
So left none elfe fhould deign to hear,
She humbly fupplicates your ear.

M 3

Imprimis. fhe fhould compliment ye;
A Venus or Diana paint ye;
Count o'er your virtues by the hunder,
And own they're more than fhe can number.
This fhe might do; but then 't would grieve
      her,
To find no mortal did believe her.
She calls you patronefs and friend,
And begs that bleffings may attend
Upon you in your humble cot,
And keep your 'fcutcheon free frae blot.
May fweet contentment, hard to find,
With radient luftre light your mind;
While numbers of your fifter train
Muft for the treafure pant in vain.

Bright Celia, with her conquering eyes,
Attempts to win the doubtful prize:
She darts a glance, ah! cruel maid,
Philander drops! a ftrapping blade.
The youth as frantic now behaves;
Of love and flames, and darts he raves.
Not Efculapius' fons can cure,
Nor eafe the pangs he muft endure.

At laſt the charmer gives conſent ;
Then Hymen does them both torment,
With nameleſs ills unknown before,
And ev'ry month augments the ſcore.

May ſtars propitious guard your life
From all the mis'ries of a wife :

Poor Delia's ſighs and tears next prove
The pains of ill requited love.
She danc'd, had wit, was wondrous fair,
And ſeem'd Alonzo's heart to ſnare.
True love and conſtancy he vow'd ;
But this by all muſt be allow'd,
That young men's tongues do not impart
The real language of their heart.
He wed another, ſad to tell !
And bad the mournful maid farewel.

O Janet, may you never know
The pangs that lovers undergo.

Cordelia too, with look demure,
Contentment wiſhes to enſure.

M 4

She flattering Cupid wont believe:
She knows that Hymen can deceive;
But fondly hopes in verfe to fhine,
Affifted by the tuneful Nine;
To call their treafures all her own,
E'en in defpite of fortune's frown.
But weak, alas! is her pretence;
Her fong proves deftitute of fenfe.
Each cavilling critic does her vex,
And ev'ry cenfure fore perplex.

O may you never feel the pain,
We heedlefs fcribbling fools fuftain.

A thoufand more from various views,
The gliding meteor fwift purfues.
The Patriot toils, in penfive mood,
For honour and Britannia's good.
The Courtier deems his Sov'reign's fmile
Would all his anxious cares beguile.
O Janet, fhun the coxing tribe,
Who barter virtue for a bribe.
The Coxcomb's care we well can guefs;
He thinks the charm confifts in drefs,

Pomatum, powder, linens white,
Wafh-balls, perfumes, and mirrors bright.
The Mifer hopes his joys to hold,
Faft lock'd within his bags of gold:
Thieves, moth and ruft, corrupt his reft;
May all his forrows be your jeft.
The plodding fage long years has fpent
In fearching for the gem content,
Which often does, I know not why,
In heaps of ruftic rubbifh lie.

And may my honeft friend juft now,
Without much queft be found by you;
May your old fhoes, your ftaff and plaidy,
Be always for the journey ready:
And blithly may ilk neighbour greet you;
May cakes, and fcones, and kibbocks meet
        you;
And may they weel ilk pocket cram,
And in your bottle flip a dram.
May your wee glafs, your pipe and fpecks,
Be ay preferv'd frae doleful wrecks.
May your wee houfe, baith fnug and warm,
Be fafe frae ev'ry rude alarm

Of wandering lovers, who'd effay
To make foft innocence their prey:
Or ruffians, caft in rougher mould,
Whofe fordid bofoms beat for gold.

Content grows joy, in meeting there
The little, lovely, blooming fair,
Who makes thy cot and thee her care;
Whofe gentle, gen'rous, noble mind,
Tho' great and rich, can here prove kind;
Whofe footfteps mark her path with peace,
Whofe fmile bids ev'ry forrow ceafe;
For age and want, and wo provides
And over mifery prefides.

Her father's worth, and mother's charms
Efteem and fond affection warms,
While kind D---f---s, with rapture fpies,
The fighing breaft and fwimming eyes;
Whofe rays have found in James and thee,
The melting charm of mifery.
That charm much more the cherub moves,
Than did his gift of cooing doves;

Whofe hearts, lefs tender than her own,
Breathe forth their ever pleafing moan.
Sweet innocence, in her we find;
Bright truth illuminates her mind:
Each action fays, for her to give
It is more joy than to receive.
Let James and you for Loudoun pray,
Whofe charms have lur'd me from my lay.

Janet farewel, you've lint and tow,
O keep your rock ay frae the low;
Tho' turmoils torture land and fea,
Content may fmoke a pipe with thee.

WHEN firſt Alcanzar to the town did
        come,
The people all believ'd that he was dumb:
In troops, with haſty ſteps, to him they went;
To get their fate preſag'd was their intent.
The man well vers'd was in the myſtic art,
And quick as thought could wondrous
        things impart.
Whoever were with anxious cares oppreſs'd,
Or on account of abſent friends diſtreſs'd,
Unto Alcanzar ſwiftly did repair,
Each of his purſe did amply make him ſhare.
It matters not how great the diſtance be,
A ſhip is rear'd, he wafts him o'er the ſea:
Tho' in diſtreſs, them frees from ev'ry pain;
Dead or alive they now muſt croſs the main:·
Bedaub'd with lace, of gold they've got great
        ſtore,
And ſwift he lands them on Britannia's
        ſhore.

The nymphs and fwains do next his aid
    demand ;
He ties them all in Hymen's filken band :
He does young Strephon with lov'd Delia blefs,
Tho' wont ere while to fhun his fond ad-
    drefs.
Sly Sanders too, who loves and woos for
    gold,
Sees Sufan's charms down on the table told :
Cows, calves and horfes, plac'd before his
    fight,
A widow rich will well his love requite.
Poor Celia next, who, for fome fickle fwain,
Spends days in forrow, and whole nights in
    pain :
It was his abfence caus'd the maid to mourn,
But fam'd Alcanzar made him foon return.
His antic geftures did the fair one cheer,
And home fhe went, releas'd from every fear.
Old Elfpa now comes trembling for her fate ;
She would be wed, but fears it is too late :
Her locks, alas ! are filver'd o'er with grey ;
Yet to Alcanzar fwift fhe takes her way.

She gave a sixpence; La lies mark the rest,
She's with a husband and five children blest.
Here maids of fifty, widows of fourscore,
May all get marri'd for a penny more.

But is the man like as his merit priz'd?
Ah no! he is by empty fools despis'd.
A crafty youth, Will Watson was his name,
Did strive to ruin great Alcanzar's fame.
He dress'd himself all in a maid's array,
Gown, stays and petticoat, extremely gay;
A muslin head-dress, with a large toopee;
Few of our Ladies look'd so fine as he.
Up street he walk'd with a majestic air,
And to Alcanzar's lodgings did repair.

First gave a penny, then he shew'd his
    hand,
And did with down cast eyes dejected stand:
But who can tell the sequel without tears?
Alcanzar's chalk too soon a cradle rears.
Who wont bewail this maid's sad decay?
She pregnant proves, her lover gone to sea.
Now all around upon the youth did gaze,
Such dismal signs had fill'd them with amaze.

Will gave a penny more; the fage did bring
The lover home, and wed them with a ring.
Eight children too, he plac'd before their
 fight
Will feem'd well pleas'd, and bade them all
 good night.

This might have pafs'd, had he the fact
 conceal'd;
But O 'twas cruel! Willy all reveal'd.
He thought indeed, but all his thoughts
 were vain,
The fam'd Alcanzar's character to ftain.
For one fpoil'd difh who would a meal de-
 fpife!
Or for one fmall miftake condemn the wife?

ALONZO TO DELIA.

TO you my fair, the emprefs of my
      heart,
I'm urg'd to vent my pure, untainted flame;
Tho' language faintly can my thoughts im-
      part,
My fwelling fighs, your kind attention claim.

See Venus felf outrival'd by your charms:
Vain my attempt thy virtues to portray
O come my darling haften to my arms
Within my bofom ftill you bear the fway.

Life without thee no pleafure can beftow;
O might my fuit thy tender pity move!
No mufe can paint the ills I undergo;
And nought can cure them but my Delia's
      love.

No bold ambitious views infpire my breaft:
And what is honour but an empty name?
While Delia fcorns, I never can be bleft,
Though founding heralds did my praife pro-
    claim.

Know, lovely charmer, that our ancient fire
Did languifh, tho' in Eden's fragrant bow'rs;
Till the firft nymph bade love his breaft in-
    fpire,
And by her prefence cheer'd the ling'ring
    hours.

But Adam's love could never equal mine,
Nor did bright Eve fuch radient beauty fhare.
O come, my darling, heart and hand refign,
And ev'ry mufe fhall hail the happy pair.

N

DELIA TO ALONZO.

—————————

WHEN Adam was in spacious Eden
                plac'd,
Where rural sweets luxuriant did abound,
All that could charm the eye or please the
                taste,
In this blest scene of happiness was found.

O'er wide creation, he an empire sway'd:
The creatures all with whom the world was
                stor'd,
His sov'reign mandates with delight obey'd,
And own'd him as their universal lord.

What would he more, to render bless com-
                plete?
You say he lack'd the sweets of social life,
Until fair Eve, with charms divinely sweet,
Became his friend, his partner, and his wife

But think, fond youth, how tranfient was
    the blifs.
Scarce had he felt the joys of mutual love,
Scarce had he once receiv'd th' ambrofial kifs,
When ah! his darling did his ruin prove!

Did fhe, who was adorn'd with ev'ry grace,
Prove fatal to the father of mankind?
Who of her daughters, a degen'rate race,
Can boaft more art the tranquil hours to bind?

To fue for better, fir, would be in vain:
None ever yet did mother Eve excel.
Be warn'd by Adam; fhun the glitt'ring train,
Left fome fond nymph your pleafures all ex-
    pel.

A fingle life we find replete with joys.
The matrimonial chain I ever dread.
A ftate of celibacy is my choice;
Therefore Alonzo never can fucceed,

DELIA TO ALONZO.

WHO HAD SENT HER A SLIGHTING EPISTLE.

————— - —————

SIR, I your letter did perufe;
   So elegant the ftyle you ufe,
Abafh'd, confounded I did mufe
        Struck with amaze;
Great wit and learning you diffufe
        In all your lays.

You've been upon Parnaffus' top,
More high than Alexander Pope;
And wild Arabia's plains you grope
        For Phenix rare,
That ufeful knowledge you may drop,
        While dunces ftare.

Your Pegafus, ftill on the wing,
More fweet than Philomel you fing ;
And fwift from diftant climes you bring
     Notes hard to read :
Does Phenix, fir, from afhes fpring ?
      'Tis ftrange indeed.

But more difficult 'tis to fcan,
That dire, deceitful creature man ;
Of all the work in Nature's plan,
     Sure none can be
So intricate to underftan',
      As myftic he.

His breaft is fill'd with mazy wiles ;
His count'nance ftor'd with fickle fmiles :
His flatt'ring fpeech too oft beguiles
     Pure innocence ;
And when he writes, his lofty ftyle's
      Replete with fenfe.

Such eloquence does merit praife ;
Deep erudition fwells your lays :

N 3

You feem the laureate of our days;
          And all the nine,
Your mighty character to raife,
          Do now combine.

'Tis pity, fir, that fuch as you
Should agriculture's paths purfue,
Or deftin'd be to hold the plough
          On the cold plain;
More fit that laurels deck'd the brow
          Of fuch a fwain.

Yet Homer's parts few did commend,
Till death his doleful days did end;
Then feven cities did contend
          A right to claim;
Each vow'd from thence he did defcend,
          So great his fame.

Perhaps, fir, in fome future age,
Struck with the beauties of your page,
Old Scotia's chieftains may engage
          Your name to raife;

More have they to excite their rage,
    Than Homer's lays.

But I muſt drop the pond'rous theme,
Leſt you my weak attempts ſhould blame;
So ſure your title is to fame,
    Who runs may read;
Of ſuch your merit to proclaim
    You have no need.

Know then, that love within my breaſt,
Has never yet been known to reſt;
Nor would I harbour ſuch a gueſt,
    To give me pain:
I wiſh you, ſir, ſo much diſtreſs'd,
    Soon well again.

FLAVIA TO CARLOS.

———————

DEAR fir, accept this miſſive ſent
    From one whoſe mind's ſincerely bent,
On ever acting ſo with you,
As ſhall evince her friendſhip true.
But how ſhall Carlos really know,
That friendſhip in her breaſt doth glow?
A friend is more than empty name:
Few juſtly can the title claim.
Were Flavia born in ſtation high,
Her friendſhip ſoon you would deſcry:
Her op'lence quickly would reveal,
What pen'ry bids her now conceal.
Then Carlos would her favour boaſt,
Nor be ſo much by fortune croſs'd.

.Thus Flavia talks of her efteem,
As heroes conquer in a dream;
Or as a culprit, doom'd to die,
In dungeon where he's forc'd to lie,
Might boaſt of what he could effect,
Were kings attentive to his beck.

You laugh, dear Sir, and pray what then,
Muſt Flavia call you beſt of men?
Muſt high encomiums grace her lays,
And all her notes be fwell'd with praife?
Know Sir, when friendſhip does commence,
All flatt'ry muſt be fpurn'd from thence:
No real friendſhip can exiſt,
In the difembling flatt'rer's breaſt.
What can poor Flavia then beſtow,
But wiſh you ſtill may better grow?
Your wit ſtill more and more refine,
And all the beauties of your min',
With radient luſtre ever ſhine;
In virtue's paths, ſtill on to tread,
Which to the fair Elyſium lead;
May every action juſtly claim
The Poet's wiſh, that thing call'd Fame.

As through life's winding vale you rove,
May ftill your ftars propitious prove,
And richeft bleffings on you fhower;
May fweet contentment grace your bower;
By love and fortune ever crown'd,
May honour all your wifhes bound.
Nor accefs find within your breaft,
One thought your friend would wifh fup-
  preft;
And may they foon at Tyburn fwing,
Who would not fign what here I fing.

MOFFAT WELL.

ON the delightful banks of Mein,
  The mufe laments in penfive ftrain;
The nymphs affembl'd on the green,
  Of Nelly's abfence all complain.

Our rural fwains no joys can find,
  But ftill in penfive filence mourn;
With heads upon the turf reclin'd
  They figh, and wifh your fwift return.

Oft have they curs'd fair Moffat town,
  With all the virtues of the Well;
The fprightly Beau, and ruftic clown,
  Of Nelly's charms delight to tell.

Dear maid, it is for you alone,
　　They spend whole days and nights in sighs;
And will you disregard their moan,
　　And all their plaintive notes despise?

'Tis Autumn now, the fertile field,
　　Rich Ceres decks with yellow grain;
With joy we would our sickles wield,
　　If Nelly deign'd to grace the plain.

Come now and of our labours share;
　　None better can that weapon ply;
O mitigate Philander's care,
　　Whose toil seems less when you are nigh.

Once more, dear Nell, I'd wish to see
　　You cheerful join the rural throng;
Your presence would enhance our glee,
　　And sweetly animate my song.

A

YOUNG LADY'S LAMENTATION

FOR THE

LOSS OF HER SISTER BY MARRIAGE.

———————

WHAT tongue can half my woes ex-
    prefs ?
What force of eloquence can tell?
The caufes of my deep diftrefs
    Are fuch as ever feem to fwell.

My parents not ignoble were;
    My father once a merchant fam'd;
But now in a fuperior fphere,
    'Mongft *landed gentlemen* he's nam'd.

My mother, of no mean extract:
    The famous Freyburgh gave her birth;
With wit and prudence ftill fhe'll act;
    None more accomplifhed on earth.

My brethren all for valour fam'd,
　　Their merit great, what pen can fhow；
Their praife has been by fame proclaim'd,
　　While juftly in efteem they grow.

I had one only fifter dear；
　　Our parents' joy and pride were we；
Our charms attractive did appear
　　To men of high and low degree：

Who often times, in foft addrefs,
　　Did ftrive our favour to obtain,
While we of fortitude poffefs'd,
　　Refus'd their offers with difdain.

They vow'd we would their ruin prove,
　　Perfifting in our cruelty；
But we were wont to laugh at love,
　　And little Cupid's darts defy.

We ever arm'd were cap-a-pee；
　　Indiff'rence was our favourite fhield；
But by fome fatal deftiny,
　　My fifter languifh'd in the field.

Depriv'd of all defenſive arms,
  (I ſigh, my tears begin to flow)
And ſlain by a ſea captain's charms,
  She married was a month ago.

In an unlucky moment he,
  From Plutus ſure had learn'd the art,
Made his empoiſon'd arrows flee,
  Till one of them did pierce her heart.

She did not wiſh to find relief,
  But an ignoble victim fell,
Which fill'd our parents' hearts with grief;
  Their ſorrows great what tongue can tell?

The balſam of advice was brought,
  With drops of ſtrict authority;
Preſcriptions ſtill to ſhun ſhe ſought,
  Nor would the medicines apply.

With water of forgetfulneſs,
  She oft was bid to bathe the wound:
The ſearch was vain, ſhe did proteſt
  This water never could be found.

It griev'd us much thus to behold
    Our counsels slighted with disdain:
His feather'd darts were tipp'd with gold,
    Which render'd every effort vain.

But conscious that our parents dear
    Could not behold the fatal blow,
To make the stroke seem less severe,
    She at a distance met the foe.

Her peerless charms she there resign'd,
    Compell'd by love's supreme command;
A clown by travels much refin'd
    Did eager clasp her beauteous hand.

I will lament a sister lost.
    Ah! ladies hear my piteous moan,
Depriv'd of what I once could boast,
    I now must keep the field alone.

What though I no assistance have,
    I hope to act courag'ously,
The subtle foe still to outbrave,
    And man's seducing arts defy.

The rich, the poor, the proud, the flave,
 The fop, the clown, the low, the tall,
The gay, the giddy, or the grave,
 I fcornfully defy them all.

O

RIVAL SWAINS.

WHILE o'er the plains ftern winter
  bore the fway,
And Sol from Capricorn diffus'd his ray,
Nigh Bolton Gate, beneath a hawthorn fhade,
Two rural fwains fad lamentations made:
Each for an abfent damfel feem'd to mourn,
While throbbing breafts did figh for figh
  return.

Young D——y's notes and T—'s fond
  praifes prov'd,
That D——h T——r was the maid belov'd.
Says D—k, " O had I thefe fweet hours again,
I've fpent with her; but ah! I wifh in vain.

The nymph is fled; to Manchester she's gone,
Nor heeds my sighs, nor yet regards my
     moan:
Her cruel aunts did contribute their aid,
To banish from my sight the lovely maid.
O little Cupid, choose two fatal darts,
And with a vengeance, send them to their
     hearts;
May they endure the agonizing pain
Of love, yet ever unbelov'd remain;
And, when far hence, by death they're
     doom'd to go,
Then let their task be leading apes below.

Young D——h was the fairest on the
     plain,
Admir'd and lov'd by ev'ry wond'ring swain.
Her charms exterior might a hero bind;
But ah! the beauty that adorns her mind,
To paint does far exceed my Muse's skill.
To you, dear T— I'll now resign the quill."
Says T—, "On her the Graces seem to wait;
Her form, how fair! enchanting is her gait.

Her youthful charms, no tongue could e'er
    exprefs;
Nor does her abfence render them the lefs.
The foft impreffion with me ftill remains;
I'm captive, yet I glory in my chains.
With fond delight I retrofpect the day,
When we to E——n took our way,
With hearts elate, to view the Scottifh fair,
Lov'd D——h fweeten'd all the pleafures
    there.
Bleft with her company upon the road,
How charming feem'd each rugged path we
    trode?
Nor could the Scottifh fair fuch charms dif-
    play;
My darling reign'd the emprefs of the day.

But ah! reflection animates my pain,
Such happy days I'll ne'er behold again.
Alas! I languifh now in deep defpair;
O that I could forget my abfent fair!"

While thefe two youths rehears'd their
    plaintive tale,
A third came ftalking o'er a diftant dale:

R——n his name, whofe anxious looks did
  fhow,
His beating bofom much opprefs'd with wo.
Of J——y's charms, he in foft concert fung;
J——y the gay, the beauteous, and the young:
She who of late, with parfon F——r ftay'd,
In the low ftation of a dairy-maid.
Yet there it was fhe gain'd young R——n's
  heart,
And in her abfence nought can eafe his fmart.

O haplefs lads! can nought allay your pain,
Till thefe two charming maids return again?
Is there none elfe can eafe your tortur'd mind?
None elfe fo fair, fo virt'ous and fo kind?
So may you think, and thus in fighs lament,
Till Hymen's fetters make you all repent.
Better bewail an abfent love for life,
Than be tormented by a fractious wife.

TO

A LADY

WHO SENT THE AUTHOR SOME PAPER

WITH A READING OF SILLAR'S POEMS.

DEAR madam, with joy I read over your
    letter;
Your kindnefs ftill tends to confirm me your
    debtor;
But can't think of payment, the fum is fo
    large,
Tho' farthings for guineas could buy my
    difcharge.
But, madam, the Mufes are fled far away,
They deem it difgrace with a milkmaid to
    ftay.

Let them go if they will, I would fcorn to
      purfue,
And can, without fighing, fubfcribe an adieu.
Their trifling mock vifits, to many fo dear,
Is the only difafter on earth I now fear.
Sure Sillar much better had banifh'd them
      thence,
Than wrote in defpite of good manners and
      fenfe:
With two or three more, whofe pretenfions
      to fame
Are flight as the bubble that burfts on the
      ftream.
And left with fuch dunces as thefe I be num-
      ber'd,
The tafk I will drop, nor with verfe be in-
      cumber'd;
Tho' pen, ink and paper, are by me in ftore,
O madam excufe, for I ne'er fhall write more.

F I N I S.

www.ingramcontent.com/pod-product-compliance
Lightning Source LLC
Chambersburg PA
CBHW020615030726
47497CB00007B/2257